# SANTA FE FORTUNE

By
Ginny Baird

Published by
Winter Wedding Press

Edited by Linda Ingmanson
Cover by Darleen Dixon

# About the Author

From the time that she could talk, romance author Ginny Baird was making up stories, much to the delight -- and consternation -- of her family and friends. By grade school, she'd turned that inclination into a talent, whereby her teacher allowed her to write and produce plays, rather than write boring book reports. Ginny continued writing throughout college, where she contributed articles to her literary campus weekly, then later pursued a career managing international projects with the US State Department.

Ginny's held an assortment of jobs, including school teacher, freelance fashion model, and greeting card writer, and has published more than twelve works of fiction and optioned nine screenplays. She's additionally published short stories, nonfiction and poetry, and admits to being a true romantic at heart.

Ginny is an award-winning writer the author of several bestselling romantic comedies, including novellas in her Holiday Brides Series. She's a member of Romance Writers of America (RWA), the RWA Published Authors Network (PAN), and the RWA Published Authors Special Interest Chapter (PASIC).

Ginny lives with her family in Tidewater, Virginia. When she's not writing, Ginny enjoys cooking, biking and just about any word game, including crossword puzzles and Scrabble. She loves hearing from her readers by email at GinnyBairdRomance@gmail.com and can also be found online at http://www.ginnybairdromance.com.

## SANTA FE FORTUNE

*"I had a really great time tonight," she said, beaming up at him and feeling very much as if it had been a date.*

*"Me too," he said, stepping a fraction of an inch closer. Sea-blue eyes washed over her, threatening to pull her under. And boy, did she want to get swept away. "I'm glad you agreed to see me tomorrow, even if it's just an arrangement."*

*Gwen sensed Dan could rearrange her heart every which way, if she wasn't careful. "I'm glad I'm seeing you too," she said, feeling the warmth in her cheeks.*

*"Ten o'clock work for you?" he asked, his tone growing gravelly.*

*"Uh-huh," she uttered, mesmerized by his gaze.*

*He moved nearer now, his mouth just inches away. "I'll be damned if I don't want to kiss you," he said, his voice a husky rasp.*

*And she'd be damned if she didn't want him to. "Dan..." she said, tilting up her chin and closing her eyes.*

*"But I won't," he said, snapping her back to attention, eyes open. "Not now. Not here. Not like this..."*

*She started to speak as he brought his fingers to her lips. "If ever I've seen a woman who deserves to be kissed well, it's you. But the timing has got to be right. You have to be sure." He cast a cursory glance at her wedding band and backed away. "I need to be sure. Something tells me we've both gone down a path neither of us wants to travel again..."*

# Chapter One

Gwendolyn Marsh leaned across the large oak table that served as a desk. "I'm going to be honest with you, Mr. Holbrook. I didn't fly all the way out here to get swindled."

Dan stared in disbelief at the incredibly contentious woman. *Swindled* was an awfully big accusation coming from such a small frame. She couldn't stand more than five foot five in heels, and she'd nearly tumbled off them striding into the place.

"Like I told you, Mrs. Marsh, I'm not in the position to make that decision. If two thousand a canvas is what Ms. Holstein quoted you in the email, then I'm afraid I'll need to stick by that."

Soft gold curls fell at uneven angles, framing a lovely face as deep brown eyes homed in on him. If she weren't so hard-edged, he might consider her beautiful. Dan stopped himself, realizing appraisals of the clientele weren't in his job description.

"It's *Ms.,* if you must know."

Some lucky fellow was off the hook.

"My apologies. I saw the wedding band and..."

"It's a relic, okay? I haven't gotten used to going without it."

"I'm sorry, I had no idea. I understand it takes a while."

She leveled him a look, as if he were the culprit. Hey, maybe in her eyes, all men were. Dan had met the type before and could easily read the signs: *steer clear, not for you buddy, a sexy woman's not everything...* Sexy? Did he just think *sexy?* Gwendolyn Marsh wasn't movie-star thin like most females here. Her formfitting sundress hugged every curve in just the right way. Wrong way, as far as he was concerned. This was just another sign he'd been alone too long. It wasn't like Dan didn't have his reasons. In fact, when he was being honest, Dan realized he was likely worse news for her than she was for him. All women after a while had hopes, dreams…and Dan Holbrook was just the man to dash them.

Dark eyes sparked with fierce determination. "I think I'd like to speak to Ms. Holstein myself."

"I'm afraid that won't be possible."

She arched one perfectly manicured eyebrow. "Why not?"

This was just what Dan needed, a hot-tempered, hot-bodied woman waltzing into his Santa Fe gallery on a hot July afternoon. Okay, it wasn't technically his gallery…

Dan cursed himself for his soft spot in agreeing to run the place while Nancy was away. He didn't even like being indoors.

"Ms. Holstein is in the south of France, will be until next month."

She pulled her naturally plump lips into a thin pink line. "I see." She faltered slightly, nearly losing her composure. There was sheen to her eyes that made them look moist. Dan hoped she wasn't about to break down crying. Nancy had assured him this would be easy, just a few clients flying in from out of state. Surprise negotiations and weepy women weren't in the mix. Negotiations Dan could handle. Weepy women were another story.

A bell tinkled above the door, and a couple of well-dressed patrons entered, a man in an expensive suit and a woman wearing a tailored dress and high-end cowgirl boots.

"Be right with you folks," Dan told them, surmising these were the buyers from Los Angeles.

Gwen stood, apparently taking this as a dismissal. "Well, I guess that's it, then." She tucked her clutch under one arm and thrust forward the opposite hand. "Thanks for your time."

Dan sent a furtive glance at the Californians perusing shelves of New Mexican pottery and pretending not to listen. "Ms. Marsh, I'm afraid we got off on the wrong…" She tapped a strappy sandal, sporting bright painted nails and multiple toe rings. Heat rose at Dan's nape as his gaze eased up shapely legs. "…foot."

She withdrew her hand and cocked her head sideways, waiting.

"What I mean is, please sit back down, and let's discuss this like reasonable people. I'm sure we can work something out." Dan cringed at the sound of his own voice. Groveling? Here was a word not even in his vocabulary, yet he was being just about as placating as humanly possible. Dan wasn't doing it for himself, he remembered. He was doing this for Nancy. Other than the day-to-day oversight of things, which really was no problem, she'd given him only two jobs to do. Surely a man as capable at cutting deals as he was wouldn't have trouble selling a few items to some Los Angeles industry execs and buying canvases from an easy-going North Carolina native. Dan had a notion Nancy had never met Gwendolyn Marsh face-to-face when she'd made the latter assessment.

The hardness lining her eyes eased just a little. "I suppose I could stay for a bit," she said, her voice taking on the lilt of the mid-Atlantic South. She took her seat, splaying the lap of her flowered sundress across tightly nestled knees.

The Californians tastefully removed themselves to the back of the gallery to study a photographic desert landscape series, and Dan sat as well. He plucked a hanky from his suit pocket and dabbed the back of his neck, thinking it had to be over a hundred degrees in here.

Something tender welled in Dan's throat, and he realized he wasn't just doing this for Nancy. For some inexplicable reason, he felt driven to be nice to Ms. Marsh for her own sake. Never mind that she'd practically bulldozed right over him crashing in here. After all, he'd dealt with worse in business before. The truth was Nancy had given him some leeway. If Marsh really pushed, Dan could go up as high as three thousand a pop, mostly because Nancy had faith in Marsh's work and thought it was good. Nancy also believed that Marsh could develop a Santa Fe following. Many of the buyers here came from the West Coast, and Marsh's oils capturing snippets of sea life would be a ready sell. Dan had seen the slides, and they were impressive. Borrowing more from impressionism than realism, Marsh had a way of zeroing in on the smallest, seemingly inconsequential detail, like an isolated seashell, and illuminating it in a special and grandiose way.

She opened her purse and withdrew a thin ledger. "If you'd let me show you my figures, I'm sure you'll understand why my prices have gone up."

Dan scanned the haphazardly arranged numbers, deciding she was no mathematician. He pointed to one clumsily assumed total. "I can understand where material costs have climbed, but how exactly is it that your hourly rate has doubled?"

"Hard times, Mr. Holbrook," she said without flinching. "Don't you read the papers?"

"*Wall Street Journal* and you?" he bantered without skipping a beat.

"Well, I…read, of course." With that, she awkwardly angled an elbow and sent her clutch crashing to the floor. "Oh no!"

A small cloud of makeup powder-puffed up from beneath them as a rolling lipstick assaulted Dan's loafer. To this day, he'd never understood the mysteries of a woman's bag.

"Here, let me," he began.

"No! I've got it!"

They bent simultaneously toward the mound of sprawled purse contents, nearly knocking heads. "I'm sorry!" he said, down on hands and knees to help her.

"My fault!"

A scent overtook him as cunning and fine as the most succulent desert flower. Dan looked up into bewitching brown eyes less than six inches away. Whatever was happening here, he had to put a halt to it. This was no sensible way for a man pushing forty to behave. He was reeling like a raving teenager. He hadn't been in a position this compromising with a woman in a while, and it showed. All sorts of crazy thoughts went racing through his head, like how it might feel to kiss her good and hard as she probably deserved.

"You guys okay over there?" a pair of cowgirl boots called from the corner.

"Thanks, we've got it!" Gwen replied, scooting back on her knees. She couldn't believe this mess! What had she gotten herself into? Here she was with this hunky beast of a man, trapped beneath a solid yet decorative desk.

He had a rugged face, tanned like he was used to working outdoors. His sandy hair held a hint of sunlight too. Toned muscles strained beneath his suit jacket as he posed on all fours, looking far more like a predator in the wild than a staid art collector. Gwen had an improbable instinct to flee but was powerless to run away. He'd been an impossible man above board, but down here in the shadows, he revealed something more. Instinct told Gwen that Holbrook was the sort of man who knew how to kiss a woman and kiss her right. She imagined getting swept into his powerful arms, his mouth moving down on hers...

"Are you all right?" His gaze dove into her as heat crept up her cheeks.

"Yes, fine. That's all, I think," she said, scooping the remainders into her clutch.

Gwen didn't know why his gorgeous stare had unnerved her so. It wasn't like she was attracted to him, for heaven's sake. If her take on Holbrook was correct, he had plenty of women falling all over him already. What would a sophisticated Western entrepreneur like him want with a Carolina girl like her anyway? Apart from a quick good time, probably not a lot, and Gwendolyn Marsh was quite done with being somebody's goodtime girl, thank you very much.

Little lines pulled at the corners of his mouth, and she realized suddenly they were still both on the floor. "If you've got all you need, don't you think we should..." He gave a thumbs-up, and she pushed back, standing awkwardly.

Holbrook brushed off his trousers, the slight tugs showing off powerfully muscled thighs. Clearly not just a gallery owner, she thought, cheeks flaming as he caught her staring.

A tense moment ensued as both appeared to forget where they were or what they were there for. As if to remind them, the California man loudly cleared his throat.

"Just finishing up," Dan told him. "Ms. Marsh," he began, addressing her.

"Gwen, please. I'd be happy if you called me Gwen." She smoothed the wrinkles from her dress and straightened the neckline.

"Gwen," he said, offering up his first true smile since she'd arrived, and boy, was it a winner. If a heartbreaker contest existed in all of the Southwest, Gwen would bet on Holbrook to take the prize. "I'm afraid I've already taken up too much of your time."

Gwen spied the California couple circling closer like sharks, apparently having grown tired of waiting, and panic set in. What a terrible two days she'd had. First, her flight to Atlanta was delayed. Then, she'd missed her Albuquerque connection, causing her to miss her originally scheduled gallery appointment. To top it off, when she finally got a replacement flight, she'd chipped a nail stuffing her bulging carry-on into the overhead compartment.

Making Santa Fe from the airport last night was easy. Finding the craftily concealed entity of Holbrook and Holstein on Canyon Road this morning proved more elusive. Even her GPS was miffed, telling her to make legal U-turns wherever possible, no matter that the prospect involved going round and round in the Vegan Market parking lot.

Now, after making a wreck of this business call, she'd be leaving here having done no business at all. Not one sale to the gallery, despite her tumultuous flight and anxiety-producing encounter with Dan Holbrook.

Gwen pulled herself up a little straighter and squared her small shoulders. She couldn't leave New Mexico without getting what she came for. Too many people depended on her, and this was the one shot she had.

"Maybe we can continue this conversation later?" she asked with a hopeful twist to her lips.

"I was just about to suggest that."

"You were?" she asked with surprise.

"Ms. Marsh…" He stopped himself. "Gwen… Do you really think Holbrook and Holstein would have had you come all this way if we didn't have a genuine interest in your work?" Crinkles formed at the corners of his blue eyes, and Gwen's heart soared.

"But I thought you said the prices quoted to me in the email were…"

"Everything in life is negotiable. Well, almost everything. Tell you what, why don't you give me a few hours to put through a phone call to France, and I'll see what I can do."

In an instant, Gwen retracted every uncharitable thought she'd had about him. When she'd first walked into the swanky, upscale warehouse and spied him double-checking the pricing on a large wall weaving, she'd imagined him incredibly stuck-up. Who wouldn't be with that six-foot build and well-proportioned frame that spoke of power and unerring self-control? She'd pegged him as the rigid sort who never took no for an answer and considered his own words the final determinant. Now that he was showing a small sliver of humanity, she realized she might have misjudged him.

"I'd love to talk again," she said, meaning it sincerely. "When's best for you?"

"How about tomorrow at lunch? Will that work?"

Ms. Holstein, his business partner, Gwen presumed, had proposed that Gwen make a little vacation out of her stay in Santa Fe while she was at it. Her sister Marian had thought it was a fine idea too. *"Go for it, Gwen! Now's your chance to finally get away!"* What Marian didn't know, and Gwen hadn't been prepared to tell her, was that Gwen's coming to Santa Fe had a whole lot to do with her.

"I'm booked at the inn for ten days," she said, smiling softly. "So, lunch tomorrow is fine."

Holbrook surprised her with a smile of his own. "Awesome." He nabbed a gallery card and quickly penned something on the back. "Let's meet here. Something tells me the conversation might flow a little better between us given a couple of avocado margaritas."

"Avocado?" she retorted, half stunned, half horrified.

Holbrook gave a genuine chuckle as she accepted his card. "Nobody's forcing the hard stuff on you. I'm sure there will be tea and soda available too."

There was a twinkle in his eye that set her tailbone tingling. Slow down there, sister, Gwen told herself. This is strictly business now. Not anywhere near a date.

"What time?" she asked primly, pinning her clutch to her side.

He studied her in an amused way. "One o'clock okay?"

"One sounds fine!" she said, scurrying toward the exit before she could do or say something absurd.

"Watch the…!"

Gwen spun toward him, noting she'd nearly upset a pretty, handblown glass vase with the edge of her bag. She grimaced, slinking out the door as the gaping Californians gawked on.

Once outside and beyond sight of the gallery's windows, Gwen snatched her bag from beneath her arm and whacked herself soundly on the forehead. Stupid, stupid, stupid. She might have blown the whole thing. And not just by breaking a priceless piece of art. The way she'd started things out had been nothing short of shameless. Crafting a confrontation with the primary gallery owner. Clearly, that could lead to nothing but butting heads.

Gwen felt a warmth surge through her, recalling their close encounter of the nearly carnal kind. There was more to Dan Holbrook than met the eye. Hadn't he just proved that with his turn of kindness at the end? But the truth of the matter was that whatever sort of man he was, or wasn't, was beside the point. Gwen had come to Santa Fe on a mission, and that mission involved dollar signs. She didn't just want the money; she needed it. Twenty thousand in cash, and she wasn't leaving New Mexico without it.

Dan finished business quickly with the couple from Los Angeles after offering sincere apologies for making them wait. They'd prearranged to purchase the desert photo series, and everything, including price negotiations, thank goodness, had been settled with Nancy in advance. It was a simple matter of the pair presenting a check and Dan providing the receipt. In the morning, he'd arrange for shipping, and Nancy's gallery assistant would be in to help with the details. That would be the simple part of Dan's day. Lunchtime could prove more problematic.

Dan chided himself for suggesting Gwen meet him at La Cantina rather than here. Outwardly, he told himself that he was being charitable. Gwen had seemed so uptight at the gallery, perhaps a more comfortable venue would be less intimidating. He'd read her résumé and understood that if she sold through Holbrook and Holstein, it would be her first real sale, her official launch in the art world. But deep in the veiled recesses of his soul, Dan suspected a slight ulterior motive. He hadn't enjoyed the company of an attractive woman in ages, and this was a safe way to do it. Lunch in the middle of the day, a straightforward business deal? What could be more innocent? Raw doubts niggled at him as he warned himself against getting in too deep. The way he'd sprung the invitation on Gwen had been completely out of character. It had been a split-second decision, an act on impulse, and Dan was anything but an impulsive man.

He would never have built his empire of custom-design homes for the moneyed set if he'd operated from a basis of anything but collected cool. In those circles, Dan was known for his keen eye and level head, as well as his effectiveness in putting together a team. From the highest-level architect to the most basic yet very skilled carpenter, every one of Holbrook Designs' workers was treated with utmost respect and handsomely paid. This was particularly appreciated in the current economic climate but had always been the operational mode for Dan. Whether times were easy or hard, Dan's business remained steady. While his homes certainly weren't cheap, they were of a consistent quality the buyer could count on. Plus, Dan was a man of his word who stood by his product. People could depend on him to deliver the best and ensure they had a comfortable and stunningly beautiful place in which to live for years to come. It was an area in which Dan felt confident, competent.

This temporary gallery-running made him feel something altogether different, and Dan didn't like it one bit. While working with the California couple had gone fine, dealing with Ms. Gwendolyn Marsh had thrown him unexpectedly off-kilter. Nancy had nowhere near prepared him for that. Just because he'd helped his big sister finance this place, that didn't mean he wanted to be involved in any intimate way. Nancy was the art history major who loved the ins and outs of acquiring art. Running a gallery in Santa Fe had always been her dream, and once Dan had found himself in a position to help with that, he'd been more than happy to foot the bill. He'd never imagined that she'd repay him by listing his name as the primary gallery owner. This perpetually led to confusion, like during his exchange with Gwen today.

No matter. He'd straighten all that out tomorrow. Surely, after a good lunch and some cordial conversation, they'd arrive at a fair compromise on price. It would be a simple matter to smooth over during coffee and dessert. Then Ms. Gwendolyn Marsh could cart her sexy little tail all the way back to North Carolina, and Dan would continue counting down the days to Nancy's return, when he would once again be free to retreat to the peaceful quiet of Paradise Ranch. Life wasn't really so complicated after all, Dan decided, thinking it through. All you needed was a plan. And Dan's plans didn't include one firecracker of a Southern belle upending his world and sending his foolish heart racing. For Dan Holbrook, days like that were done. His throat ached at the memory. He swallowed hard, trying to force it back down. Dan had stepped into the fire once and had come out barbequed. No need to start poking at coals again.

Gwen sat on the patio of her airy suite, surrounded by sweeping adobe walls, potted ferns, and cactus flowers. Despite the record-high temperatures, the lack of humidity made it pleasant enough to stay outdoors in the shade. She sipped at her host's complimentary glass of chardonnay, knowing she needed to be cautious. At seven thousand feet above sea level, one glass of wine could feel like two. The inn's cocktail hour had also offered a selection of fruits, vegetables, and cheeses, and Gwen had fixed herself a small plate as a buffering against the booze. She'd have to remain mindful of herself tomorrow at lunch, particularly in light of the proposed margaritas.

Gwen couldn't help but feel a slight tingle of hopeful anticipation. For the first time in as long as she remembered, she'd be eating out with an eligible man. She knew, of course, that it was just an art deal, and she was merely passing through town. It was nonetheless hard to deny the tiniest fluttering in her tummy that sprang to life each time she recalled being face-to-face on the floor with the undeniably handsome Holbrook. Had something authentic actually passed between them, or had Gwen been so nervous and delusional as to have imagined the whole thing?

She glanced down at the simple gold band on her left ring finger. Gwen wasn't sure if it was her marriage she couldn't forget or her failure to maintain it. *"Marshes aren't quitters!"* her mom, Elizabeth, had always said. While life may have quit on Elizabeth, she wasn't about to let her daughters give up on anything. It was a mantra burned into them, her and her sister Marian both. Gwen only wished Marian had quit having babies about three children ago. Marian was expecting her sixth, and after years of verbal and physical abuse, her alcoholic husband, Tom, had finally run out on her. Gwen had truthfully considered this a blessing, as it had been clear after the first couple of years that Marian never intended to leave Tom.

Marian worked part-time as a hospital nurse and tried to get the day shift as much as possible. When she was gone, she left her oldest, the eleven-year-old, in charge. During night shifts, her elderly neighbor, Ms. Tilly, helped out. During the academic year, Marian had daycare arranged for the twins while the others were in school. She wasn't sure how she'd manage once the new baby came along, especially under the threat of losing her home. Marian's mortgage was several months overdue, and the collectors were moving in. She hadn't told Gwen that Tom stopped sending payments, or that she was in so deep, until it was almost too late. As it was, Marian barely had funds in her meager savings account to buy a few months' worth of diapers. Her checking account was essentially empty, being worn down month after month by her family's needs, including the kids' doctors' bills.

Marian had been in tears when she'd told Gwen the truth. If she lost her house, she feared her children would be taken away from her. She had nowhere else to go. Gwen's sparse two-bedroom could scarcely hold them all, not for any length of time, at least. And their mom, having long ago been placed in the memory-care unit of a retirement home, was far from being able to help. She barely scraped by on Social Security and most days didn't recognize either of her daughters, besides.

If Marian could just hang on one more year until the twins were in school, she thought she could make it. With only the new baby to place in daycare, she'd be able to work full-time. That would give her benefits like a retirement pension and health insurance. She'd be better able to meet her kids' medical expenses as well as plan for her own future. As it stood, she had six months of back mortgage to pay and another twelve months' obligation to look forward to. She was overwhelmed and in pieces, unsure of what to do. Taking Tom to court wasn't an option. Marian didn't have the financial resources, and even if she did, it would be hard squeezing blood from a stone. Tom was on and off the bottle and in and out of work. She couldn't rely on him now any more than she had during their marriage.

It was a dire and depressing situation. Gwen had thought for weeks about what she might do to help her sister. The trouble was Gwen was in financial strife herself. Robert had been so furious at her for kicking him out, he'd run up over ten thousand dollars in credit-card debt on purpose. The pro bono women's shelter attorney Gwen consulted said there was nothing Gwen could do about Robert maxing out the account jointly held in their names.

Gwen was unfortunately just as liable for half of his debts as entitled to half of his earnings. Good luck with that. Robert, a successful production assistant with a Hollywood company providing East Coast sets, had found plenty of loopholes in which to stash his cash. Gwen twisted the simple wedding band once, realizing her cheeks were damp.

She finished off her chardonnay, more determined than ever to sell those canvases and at the best possible price. She'd started small with a few local juried art shows around town, then had dared to put a modest portfolio of slides together and began sending it out. Holbrook and Holstein in Santa Fe had been her first real nibble. In effect, it had been a really big bite. Top dollar for her work, plus the cost of round-trip air tickets and accommodations to boot. Holbrook probably thought that Gwen was being greedy, trying to barter up the price for her own gain. Nothing could be further from the truth. Marian's kids needed their mama, and Gwen needed to help her baby sister. One way or another, Gwen was going to see this through. Dan Holbrook could think anything about her that he liked. She'd never see him again after tomorrow anyway.

# Chapter Two

When Dan got to La Cantina, Gwen had already arrived. He spied her seated at a table for two in the large atrium styled like a Spanish courtyard and decorated in colorful tile. She studied the menu as he approached, a white peasant blouse sweeping her shoulders, hair pinned up in a casual way that offset her cheekbones and fair complexion. Dan had to stop walking and catch his breath. She was truly a beautiful woman, even more beautiful than he'd given her credit for yesterday at the gallery. Then again, yesterday at the gallery, she'd appeared primed to bite his head off. Today, she just looked hungry.

"Can I help you find a table, sir?" a tall waiter in a waistcoat inquired.

"Thanks, I see where I'm going," Dan said, shaking the reverie. Hearing their exchange, Gwen looked up at him and smiled. He felt a little twist in his gut and realized this was worse than he thought. Dan smiled back pleasantly, determined to pull himself together. He envisioned a large Weber grill, coals searing beneath its grate, and suddenly felt driven to thirst.

He joined Gwen at the table, exchanged pleasantries, then took a long drag of water from the glass that had been provided at his place. She eyed him curiously as he drained it all.

"It's murder out there," he said, referencing the weather.

"Certainly is hot," she agreed.

"I hope you found this place okay."

"Oh yes, just fine." Warm brown eyes sparkled enticingly.

"They've got some really great specials today. Have you taken a look?"

Gwen turned over the menu in her hands, and he wondered again about that wedding band. How long had she been divorced, and why would she continue to wear it? Dan reminded himself that delving into Gwen's personal affairs was none of his business.

She surveyed the ample list of entrees. "Any recommendations?"

"Depends on whether you like spicy."

She gave him a big, appealing grin. "I love spicy food. All kinds. But I'd love to try something particular to the region." Why did she have to look so darned likable today? She really wasn't cooperating in encouraging Dan to keep his distance.

"Would you like me to order for us?" he asked, wanting to be helpful yet not wishing to overstep his bounds.

"That would be nice. Thanks." Gwen lowered her face to her menu to disguise a faint blush.

Dan fought a swell of heat, surmising there wasn't enough air in here. "Okay, be honest with me. Yes or no to avocado margaritas?"

"You weren't kidding, were you?" she asked with surprise.

"I may be many things, but I'm not really much of a kidder."

She stared at him intently, trying to read him. Dan tried to repress a smile but felt his eyes crinkle just the same.

"That was kidding, wasn't it?" she asked, waving a scolding finger.

He let loose a belly laugh, enjoying himself. "I'm afraid it was."

Gwen released a tiny puff of air, apparently relieved. "I'll try an avocado margarita," she answered, "but just one."

A little while later, Gwen took her first taste of the tantalizing southwestern treat. Finely pureed like a smoothie, it was silky, cool, and delicious. You couldn't taste the tequila at all. Gwen was glad she'd made the advance decision to stick with one. Holbrook did too. He ordered them a delicious chicken poblano over Mexican rice, with a cold gazpacho soup to start. It was a perfect meal, and he had been right. After a couple of margaritas, their conversation flowed a lot more smoothly. For one thing, she learned that while his name was on it, he didn't actually run the gallery. He was merely filling in this month for his older sister Nancy. His real work involved home building of some kind. It was a job he seemed to enjoy and which often kept him outdoors.

"I insist that you call me Dan," he said as their plates were cleared. "Mr. Holbrook hardly seems right with me calling you Gwen. You're making me feel like an old man."

"Oh, I suspect you're not that old," she said, feeling as if she was flirting.

He colored slightly around his open collar. "Thirty-nine next month. Practically over the hill."

He was dressed casually today, in khaki slacks and an azure polo shirt that complemented his eyes. The shirt fit him nicely, stretching evenly across his broad and muscled chest. Gwen found herself wondering what it would be like to press her hands against it, feel the strength and power there. Maybe that margarita was getting to her after all.

"Well, I'm thirty-two, so not that far behind you."

He took a long, slow sip of his drink, surveying her over the rim of his glass. "Something tells me it will be some time before Ms. Gwendolyn Marsh makes it over that hill."

Now was he flirting with her? The way he studied her made Gwen think Dan had more than painting on his mind. She imagined removing his shirt and applying a deep massage oil, stroking the musculature there. Heat welled within her, sending electric currents from her fingertips to her toes. Gwen reminded herself to stay on track. Maybe the margarita was getting to him as well. Although that seemed difficult to believe, given his sturdy and scrumptious build. Oh dear, there she went again. It was a relief when Dan changed the subject by suggesting dessert. Anything to take her mind off further explorations of that come-hither chest.

"It was a wonderful lunch, but I honestly don't have room for more."

"Not even jalapeño custard pie?" Dan tempted. Gwen had the sense that Dan Holbrook could tempt even the most sensible woman into almost anything.

"Maybe next time," she said, combating a new rush of heat with a long drink of water, which, instead of hitting her lips, splashed in her lap. "Oh dear!" Gwen brought her palms to her cheeks as Dan sprang from his chair.

"Take mine," he said, pressing his cloth napkin to her skirt. Suddenly, his warmth spread through her nether regions. She gasped, and he glanced up, their eyes locking.

"I'll get it, thanks," she stammered as he pulled his napkin aside, and she took to the task with hers, promptly dropping her napkin on the floor. "My goodness."

Dan scooped low to retrieve the soggy rag. He hesitated briefly to study her dangling ankle bracelet, then righted himself slowly, his sky-blue gaze grazing hers.

Dan reddened as he handed Gwen back her napkin. "I'll call the waiter over and ask for more."

"Don't bother," she said sweetly. "I think that's got it."

Gwen couldn't believe what a klutz she'd been. What was it about this man that made her all butterfingered? Okay, the truth was Marian had sometimes accused her of being a teensy bit clumsy, but she'd never been an out-and-out wrecking ball like this. It was probably a combination of things. Her mission for money complicated by Dan's inexcusable hotness. She found herself wishing briefly that his sister Nancy had been here to meet with her instead. A split-second later, she realized that was a lie.

The hard fact was Gwen was attracted to Dan. Seriously attracted. And perhaps he'd given indications that he was the slightest bit interested in her as well. But what was wrong with that? Colleagues could enjoy a simple flirtation, for heaven's sake. Gwen was sure it happened all the time. That certainly didn't mean it had to go anywhere. Gwen hadn't come to Santa Fe to find a man. She'd come to launch her art career and help her sister. Over time, she'd also be helping herself. After a while, she could do less and less of her day job and more of what gave her pleasure and caused her spirit to soar.

"You know," Dan said as coffee arrived for the two of them. "I've gone on at length about my work, and you haven't really talked about yours. Have you been painting long?"

"I did a bit in high school, but then sort of let it go."

"How's that?" he asked.

"When I started applying to colleges, my mom encouraged me to pursue something a bit more practical." She shrugged, resigned. "She may have had a point. I'm not sure what sort of job I might have gotten as an art major. I couldn't imagine teaching something I loved so much and found so personal. I'm afraid it would have taken the passion out of it for me. So I decided to finish in music instead."

"Music?" he asked with surprise. "Are you talented?"

"Not in the least," she said with a laugh. "In fact, do you know that expression?"

Dan grinned. "Those who can, do; those who can't, teach?"

"Precisely. I can't carry a tune in a bucket, and I'm impossibly inept on the keyboard."

Dan leaned forward on his elbows. "Then how…?"

"Oh, I have a great ear for things. I mean, when someone else is doing the playing, I can pluck the mistakes right out. Not that I'm hard on my students. I'm really a very encouraging teacher." And she was too. The children appeared to love her, and their parents praised her abilities. Gwen was just thankful that none of them had borne witness to her botchery of university piano recitals. It was a blessing that she could graduate in teaching without having to prove her own exceptional skill.

Dan gave a delighted chuckle. "What grades do you teach?"

"Elementary during the school year. In the summertime, I take private piano students on, all ages up to adults."

"So you could teach me?" he asked invitingly. Uh-oh, there he went, flirting again. Gwen doubted very seriously that she could teach the dangerously capable Dan Holbrook anything. At thirty-eight, he was bound to have seen a bit of the world and more than his share of women. Gwen reminded herself not to be foolishly flattered by his probably practiced attentions.

"I'm not sure about that. Something tells me you might not be the most cooperative student."

Dan raised his brows in surprise, then released another belly laugh. "You've probably got me there. Nancy tried to teach me 'Chopsticks' once when I was ten, and I never quite got through it."

Gwen couldn't help but soften at his self-effacing honesty. If she wasn't careful, she was going to start liking the man, and that might cloud her judgment in any business dealings. She finished her coffee, realizing lunch was nearly over and they'd not yet talked turkey.

"Some people have more natural talent than others," she said kindly.

"Like you do for painting, for instance," he said, turning the conversation in what Gwen hoped would be the right direction.

"I appreciate you thinking so," she said, feeling her heart warm. "I really enjoy what I do. The thought that it might also bring happiness to someone else is just wonderful."

"When did you start painting again?"

"Oh, I did it off and on. Just for me, you know. Could never entirely let it go over the years. Then on my thirtieth birthday, my little sister, Marian, gave me the most beautiful gift, a completely new set of oils and brushes. I'd been getting by with old things, mostly cast-offs from the school art teacher who'd been sympathetic to my cause."

"Marian must know you very well."

"We're super close," Gwen said, feeling the burn in her throat. "The gift was extra special because oils are expensive, and Marian… Well, she…she doesn't have a lot of money."

"So that's when it really started? When you began painting more regularly?"

Gwen nodded, willing away the unpleasant memory of Robert coming in and upending her very first seascape. *"Ridiculous,"* he'd said. *"Where do you think you'll get with that? You sure as hell can't sing. What makes you think you can paint?"*

Gwen blinked, briefly turning away. When she turned back to Dan, she found herself caught up in his sky-blue gaze. The way he looked at her was soothing, as if he had all the time in the world to listen to what she had to say, and like none of it was ridiculous.

"I did start painting more then, yes. It was easier without the resistance."

"Resistance?"

"That doesn't really matter anymore," she said, forcing a smile. "I found a way to move beyond it."

"And the clients at Holbrook and Holstein will be glad. I assure you."

"I'm glad you brought that up so I didn't have to."

He looked at her earnestly. "Gwen, I've had a great time at lunch with you, really I have. But I have no illusions about why a beautiful young woman like you would spend time with a washed-up old bachelor like me."

Gwen blushed at the compliment but wasn't about to let herself get derailed by his manly attentions. As long as he'd started the ball rolling, she needed to push it along. "You underestimate yourself, Dan. But it's good to know you've reconsidered underestimating my work."

His gaze filled with admiration. She was being a little saucy, and he apparently liked it. "I spoke with Nancy like I promised. Holbrook and Holstein is prepared to set a fair price for your art. We can't quite go up to four thousand, but if you're willing to agree to three-five, we think we can cut a deal."

The way he'd said that made it almost seem real, as if this was actually going to happen for her. Gwen tried to contain her excitement. "Excellent," she said, giving him what she hoped was a warm, even smile. "I'm open to discussing that."

"Of course, I'm sure you're familiar with how things work," he continued. "Gallery sales are commission based, so whatever price we arrive at is provisional."

The corners of Gwen's mouth took a downturn. The fact was, she didn't know this at all. "I'm sorry. I'm not sure what you're saying."

Dan set his empty coffee cup aside and laced his fingers together in a sincere fashion. "I'm saying the gallery takes a commission. That's how it stays in business. Your work for sale there is basically on consignment."

The shock and horror hit her in the stomach like a sucker punch. "Consignment? But nothing in Ms. Holstein's email said anything about—"

His gaze softened, genuinely apologetic. "I'm sorry, Gwen. She probably thought you knew. Most of the artists we deal with are...experienced."

Gwen felt a flash of anger, but she quelled it, realizing nobody had intentionally tried to mislead her. "Are you saying I won't be getting any money now?" she asked, trying to mask the desperation in her voice.

"Now?" he asked, as if he'd never considered the possibility. "You mean, like during your ten-day trip to Santa Fe?

"Gwen, we're dealing with a process, here. We agree on what we think a reasonable buyer might pay in this market. That is the sale price. The two of us sign a contract, and then you ship the canvases. Once they're here, we hang them up for sale. As money comes in, it's funneled directly to you, less the gallery's twenty-percent commission."

Gwen felt her entire world crumbling in on her. Maybe it was her fault, hoping for too much in just one visit. But what if things didn't sell? What if enough money didn't come on time? What if the bank failed to extend its credit?

Gwen thought of Marian and her kids, of lives pulling apart... Of Robert's repeated infidelities... Her art box being tossed into the ocean... Something cut loose inside, and she felt like she might lose it at any second, break down sobbing on this already soppy napkin. She opened her purse and pulled out a tissue.

Dan reached a steadying hand across the table and laid it on hers. "Gwen? Are you all right?"

"Excuse me," she said, dabbing the corner of her eye. "I'll be right back."

Dan sat there for the longest time, wondering what he'd done wrong. Could Gwen truly have thought she'd fly out of here in just over a week with wads of cash lining her pockets? Were her circumstances really that bad? She'd seemed so fragile when she'd rushed out of here, as if she might break apart at any minute. Dan had no idea what sort of situation she was in, but he did know one thing. If he could, he wanted to help.

After what seemed like an eternity, Gwen resurfaced, all fresh-faced with newly applied lipstick and powder. Dan was finally starting to understand why women kept so much nonsense in their purses. It was for emergency situations like this.

"Any better?" he asked with concern.

She gave a sniff and lifted her chin.

"Allergies. Never know when they're going to hit me."

"Glad you're okay."

"Yes," she said, taking her seat. "Just fine, thanks." She noted the credit card receipt on the table. "Oh, you've already paid the bill. I'm sorry. I didn't mean for you to—"

"My pleasure," he said, meaning it. He hadn't had a lunch this interesting with a woman in a decade. Everything he'd learned about Gwen had been fascinating. But what intrigued him most was all that he didn't know. "Gwen," he began, hoping to broach the subject lightly. "I couldn't help but notice you were a little…thrown by our arrangement."

"The consignment, you mean?" she asked proudly. "Oh no, I knew all about it. I suspected that's how things went." It was a brave cover, but Dan saw straight through it. Didn't help her that her chin still trembled slightly.

"That's how it normally goes," he answered. "But there's really no need for us to go getting all bogged down in normalcy, wouldn't you say?"

She knitted her delicately sculpted brow. "I'm sorry? I'm not sure I follow."

A few gold tendrils broke free from their pins and spilled forward. Dan had an idiotic impulse to reach out and sweep them back, chancing a touch of her alabaster skin. He stopped himself just in time, tucking away the bill receipt in his pocket instead. "How soon can you get your canvases out here?"

"To Santa Fe? Why, in just a few days. They're all packaged and ready to ship."

"That settles it, then," he said with a wide, easy grin.

"Settles what? I haven't signed any contract."

"No, but if you will, I have an idea," he said slyly.

"What sort of idea is that?" she whispered, angling forward.

Dan looked straight in her eyes with calm reassurance. "We don't normally operate this fast, but I do have a list of potential buyers I can contact."

Her face lit up like the most stunning sunrise. "Are you saying what I think you are?"

"If fortune smiles on us, we might be able to sell a canvas or two before you leave."

"All five?" she asked with a hopeful glow.

Dan feared he'd done the wrong thing, caused her to think it was a certainty that this would go off. But when she'd gone all weepy on him, it had been impossible for Dan to stop himself. The truth was he had the means to buy all five of Gwen's canvases himself without even making a dent in his money-market account. But that would make the dealings between them personal, and Dan had vowed to keep things on a professional level.

Dan returned her gaze with cautious determination. "Let's not go pushing our luck," he said, sensing he'd gotten in over his head. He envisioned a huge, raw T-bone getting tossed onto a grill. Perspiration built at his brow, and he lifted Gwen's soggy napkin from the table to dab it.

"I need to get back to work," he said, standing and helping Gwen with her chair. "Think you might stop by later to sign the papers? The gallery closes at eight. That would be a good time."

"Eight o'clock it is," she said with a smile that knocked his socks off and held potential to knock other items of clothing off too.

Dan said a polite good-bye, then hustled out of there like a rabbit being hunted by a pack of wild coyotes. He needed to get his head together and figure his way through these next few days. Not that this should be a problem for a take-charge guy like him who knew how and where to draw the line.

Dan knew it was for the best, and really in Gwen's interest, for him to back off from any sort of romantic notions now, while the backing was good. No matter what

*Santa Fean* magazine said about Dan being the "Best Billionaire Bachelor Catch in the West," privately he knew his shortcomings would give even the most understanding woman pause. Dan had been down that dusty trail once and was determined never to go there again. Didn't matter what sort of attractive filly came out of the gate. The fact of the matter was Dan wasn't riding.

# Chapter Three

Gwen left the restaurant by exiting onto the main plaza, an oasis of green in the earth-toned adobe town. Huge shade trees lined its crisscrossing sidewalks, dotted with wrought-iron benches and lampposts. Bordered by the nation's oldest public building, the Palace of Governors, on one side and an array of upscale shops on the others, it was the city's central gathering spot and playground, complete with a bandstand in which an impromptu flautist played. Gwen strode past a snow-cone vendor and a couple of quesadilla carts on her way to explore the smattering of handmade goods the locals had spread on the ground atop woven blankets. She surveyed the assorted silver jewelry, accented with turquoise, and small trinkets for sale with an appreciative eye, and made complimentary small talk with the Native American and Mexican peoples proudly showcasing their wares.

A warm breeze blew as the sun angled high, bathing Santa Fe in its rosy glow, the impressive Sangre de Cristo Mountains just visible in the distance, their highest peaks capped with snow, even in summertime. Gwen made her way up a side street to visit Saint Francis Cathedral, a stunning Romanesque Revival structure challenging the surrounding adobe architecture with its sweeping arches and brightly hued stained-glass windows.

Perspiration dampened her hairline as she climbed the steps to the building's entrance. It was warmer in the sunlight, the scarcely filtered ultraviolet rays bearing down on her, causing her feet and hands to swell. At once, the thin gold band on her left ring finger felt too tight. She twisted it slightly as she continued her ascent toward the cathedral's front door. Gwen hadn't prayed for anything in a long time. In fact, she hadn't been to church since Robert left. Maybe she should have. Thinking it over, she understood she had much to be thankful for. Not least among her blessings was her opportunity to come here.

Gwen passed through the enormous wooden door, her senses immediately engulfed by burning incense. Though she wasn't Catholic, she didn't believe God would mind if she took a spot on a pew for a few moments to mull through her life. What an event it had been. There'd been so much to it she'd never seen coming. When she met Robert in college, he'd appeared so promising. He was ambitious and fun and seemed poised to carve out a good life for himself and any lady lucky enough to join him. When he'd asked Gwen to marry him just before graduation, she'd been over the moon. He had a good job offer in Wilmington, and they could settle in the nearby town where Gwen had grown up and her family still lived. It had all seemed so idyllic at first.

Gwen glanced down at the completely ineffectual wedding ring as her hand rested in her lap. It hadn't taken long for Robert to find someone he thought more intelligent and interesting than her. She bored him to tears with her tales of kids in school and had no real talents as far as he could gather. The people he worked with were insightful, intuitive, interesting… Maybe if Gwen looked more at the papers or followed the news, she'd be interesting too, though he kind of doubted it.

Gwen heaved a sigh, knowing she couldn't continue to beat herself up over Robert's shortcomings. When she was thinking clearly, as Marian often encouraged her to do, she understood that her marriage falling apart had more to do with him than her. Or perhaps it was due to them both and the fact that, once they'd escaped from the cocoonlike sanctuary of the university, neither of them truly fit together. Gwen wondered sadly if she was destined to fit together with any man. Perhaps that wasn't in the cards for her, and maybe that was okay. If her art took off and she built herself a career, something that she adored and was really proud of, that might be enough.

She considered her meeting this evening with Dan, realizing she'd been acting like a silly schoolgirl. It wasn't his fault she hadn't dated since her divorce, so why should she hold him accountable for her surging hormones? Any nice-looking man who'd paid her attention would likely have made her feel the same. As an elementary schoolteacher, she simply hadn't had much opportunity for that. All the men she met were either married or formerly married and quickly reattached. It seemed the decent ones didn't last long on the market. From what she'd gathered from her quick perusals of Internet dating sites, the perpetual bachelors all seemed to have something wrong with them. Then again, Dan appeared normal. Exceedingly normal, healthy, and sexually enticing as well. So why hadn't a tamale-hot catch like him been snapped up already?

Gwen decided to head back to the inn to cool off for a few hours before her gallery appointment. This praying business didn't seem to be going too well. She thought she'd probably done it wrong. It had been such a while, she couldn't tell. In any case, she was grateful to Dan for granting her this chance. At the heart of it, Gwen understood that was all this really was, a chance to sell some of her art to a very fine place and hopefully help turn her sister's life around. That was worth a few amens, no doubt. She dipped her head, offering them quickly, and bowed out of the cathedral before anyone could stop her and ask her for money. That was one part of going to church she hadn't forgotten. There was a lady near the door collecting donations for the restoration fund. Gwen slipped silently past her and out into the sunshine before the woman could hold up a brochure. Maybe once Gwen was rich and famous she'd feel a bit more philanthropic. At the moment, she scarcely had cash for dinner. She'd have to hurry to catch the wine-and-cheese hour before the other guests cleaned out the Havarti.

Dan paced the redwood-pine floors, double-checking the time on his BlackBerry. The afternoon couldn't have dragged out more if he'd planned it. It all seemed to go in slow motion, as if he were deep-sea diving, arms and legs battling against ocean pressure.

The occasional browsers stopped by, and there was the shipment to get out to Los Angeles, but Nancy's assistant Megan had come in to see to that. She wore a nose piercing and a puckish haircut that added to her image of a small sprite sprinting around the gallery. Dan had never seen a twenty-three-year-old with so much energy. She was very astute though, her nimble mind eager to acquire anything and everything about gallery running. She hoped to manage a place of her own one day and apparently did some sort of printmaking on the side.

"That's it, then," Megan said, peering up at him through heavily mascaraed eyes. "Think that I might sneak out early? I've got a date for drinks at Nines." Nines was the hipster bar on an adobe rooftop overlooking the mountains.

"Don't let me hold you back," Dan said.

"Are you all right?" Megan asked. "You've seemed a little…off this afternoon. Maybe you should head out early too."

Dan was more than a little off; he was distractingly discombobulated. He'd spent over three hours poring through Nancy's customary client list, trying to discern those who might be interested in Gwen's work. If he'd had his head on straight, the task might have taken him forty-five minutes. Instead, he'd caught himself daydreaming at every turn, reliving his lively lunch with Ms. Gwendolyn Marsh. Just as in the gallery the day before, he'd been sucked in by the feminine scent of her. Didn't help one iota that she obviously perfumed her legs, legs that were attached to one knock-out of a womanly body, teamed with a damnably adorable and kissable, he couldn't help but reason, face. And, when her eyes sparked with delight at the thought that he might help her, could actually sell her canvases in this absurd ten-day timeframe, Dan's heart had done an unexpected flip-flop.

"I'm fine," he lied to Megan. "Why don't you go on ahead? I've got an artist stopping by at closing. I'll lock up."

Megan grabbed her colorful straw bag that looked large enough to hold a weekend wardrobe and pranced out the door.

Dan strode to the desk and withdrew Gwen's contract from the nearby filing cabinet. He glanced through the folder for maybe the tenth time today, ensuring everything was in order. The paperwork was all lined up. Now all Dan had to do was steel his heart. He was getting far too carried away with this. Just because Gwen looked like an angel and spoke in a sweet Southern twang that was sexy as sin, that didn't mean he'd have to give in to her. He was a rational man, by all accounts, savvy at business dealings and skilled at keeping his emotions in check.

Okay, he'd made that one mistake. But it wasn't like it was going to come back to haunt him. It had been more than a month now, and he'd heard nothing further about it. It had been a harsh lesson in letting sleeping dogs lie. Once you make a pact to move on, there should be no looking back. Looking ahead wasn't sounding so safe at the moment either. Gwen was scheduled to be in town only ten days. She had her life back East to lead, and Dan had his own ghosts to contend with here. He shook off a gloomy feel, determined to make the best of their meeting. Dan was sensible enough to know he could assist a damsel in distress without falling into bed with her. And just to make certain he hadn't forgotten, the fates had pressed a branding iron to his chest a mere six weeks ago to drive that message home.

Gwen tugged at the zipper of her skirt, sliding it up her ample hip. She'd put on a few pounds since her divorce but still looked okay, she supposed. She'd never been accused of being overly thin. Marian was the slight one in the family, while Gwen fought the perpetual battle of the booty. Breasts, hips, and thighs had a will of their own. No matter how she tried, they relished maintaining their prefab form. After a while, Gwen had just given up and decided to enjoy life. As long as she operated within reason, didn't diet or exercise too much, she could stay within the same five-pound range that she'd grown accustomed to and certain men seemed to appreciate.

Gwen flushed at the memory of Dan's sky-blue gaze. At first she'd thought he'd just been flattering her, trying to put a gallery contact at ease. But the more she pondered it, the less she thought so. As they'd sat there discussing canvas pricing, his heated perusal had washed all over her like the clearest Caribbean wave. Gwen imagined the two of them on a distant beach, Dan bare-chested in the sun. He'd tell her once more how beautiful she was, and, half-naked in her tummy-control swimsuit, she'd feel forced to believe it. He'd take her by the waist then, pull her soft body to his, taut stomach muscles tensing as he wrapped his arms around her... Gwen heard the surf crash, water swirling furiously at their feet, as he brought his glorious mouth to hers.

Suddenly, she realized she'd stalled in applying her lipstick and was standing there all puckered up like a ridiculous guppy. "That's the price I pay for that second Shiraz," she scolded herself, vowing to make coffee. She was glad the suite's miniature kitchen supplied what she needed for that. Now where was the sugar cube she could find to quell her outlandish fantasies?

Gwen had considered putting on a flirty dress for her meeting with Dan tonight but now worried that might send the wrong message. She wasn't seeing him for any sort of social reasons, she reminded herself. They were convening to sign a contract, for heaven's sake. Gwen lifted her perfume bottle and spritzed her neck, wrists, and the backs of her knees with its fine aroma.

Gwen's belly warmed as she recalled how Dan had hesitated by her foot just an instant too long in retrieving her dropped napkin. If he'd touched her then, even by accidentally brushing her calf, she would have fainted. They would have had to call in the rescue squad to scoop her limp form off the New Mexican tile. It didn't take an expert to see the super-studly Dan Holbrook held more masculinity in one pinkie than the pallid and self-possessed Robert contained from head to toe.

Coffee, Gwen reminded herself, noting by the clock on the nightstand it was almost time. The sooner she got this over and done with, the better. If she could negotiate the paperwork without chancing to shake Dan's hand, all the better. Even after the coffee, Gwen didn't trust herself to touch him. This was what Marian called an unwelcome consequence of celibacy.

Gwen adjusted her bra, shifting her bosom into its proper place, then, quite as an afterthought, she was sure, gave her cleavage the tiniest little burst of Midnight Jasmine perfume.

Dan looked up as the door chime sounded. There she stood, looking as gorgeous as a desert sunset, the colors of her sexy, short dress swirling about her in mauve, gold, and russet browns. "Are you ready for me?" she asked, dark eyes sparkling with anticipation.

Dan thought he was, in fact had prepared for her all afternoon, but now he felt as awkward and uncertain as a teenager. "Of course," he said, working to get the words out in a businesslike manner. "Come on in." Her womanly scent overtook him as his eyes trailed from her ankles to her cleavage to her faintly colored cheekbones. "Please, have a seat." He indicated a spot, nearly missing his own chair. Dan scooted onto it as she pulled hers in toward the desk just a tad too close. The sweet angles of her knees pressed into his ever so slightly.

A crimson blush warmed her shoulders and swept up her delicate throat. "Oh! Oh my goodness. I'm so sorry!" she cried, backing up.

"No worries! Really," he protested.

Gwen sat up a little straighter in her chair and crossed her legs as Dan opened the file in front of him. He passed her the paperwork with an appreciative gaze.

"You look lovely tonight," he said, unable to stop himself.

Gwen met his eyes, her cheeks still aglow. "Thank you. You look…really super too."

Dan reined himself in, applying his best businesslike tone. "I believe everything's in order there," he said as she fanned through the pages. "If you'd like to look it over, I can answer any questions."

The sun dipped low outside, casting a tangerine hue throughout the wide-open spaces of the gallery as Gwen sorted through the agreement. After a few moments of studied concentration, she addressed Dan with a relieved smile. "It all seems straightforward." She'd worried it might be complicated, filled with legalese and fine-print sections. On the contrary, it basically laid out what they had discussed at lunch, with a few boilerplate clauses she supposed were included in most contracts of this kind. "Where do I sign?"

Dan indicated the line, then added his own signature to the page.

"Have you come up with any contacts? I mean, people who might buy my art?"

Dan smiled indulgently. "Don't you think we ought to get it here first?"

"Right! I'll have Marian send it out tomorrow. Like I said, it's all boxed and ready to go. All she has to do is call for shipping."

Dan wrote some numbers on a small notepad on the desk. "This is our account number for Southwest Express. Have your sister call this phone number and bill it to us. She can let them know where and when to pick up the packages."

"Well, thanks, that's very gracious. That will help a lot." Gwen couldn't let him know that her wallet was paper-thin or that her sister was destitute.

"I've actually already sent out a couple of emails, feelers, if you will, to gallery contacts who might have an interest in an East Coast ocean scene or two."

Gwen felt her face warm with excitement. "That's wonderful!" She fought an urge to race around the desk and hug him.

"As soon as the pieces arrive," he continued, "I'll start making follow-up calls. I'm hoping to have some serious buyers in looking by the end of the week. Assuming the shipment goes as planned."

Gwen sprang from her seat and lunged for his hand. "I don't know how to thank you," she said, taking his hand in hers and holding it firmly.

His gaze wrapped around her, trapping her in his heat. "It's my pleasure, really," he said, exerting delicate pressure against her palm. Little tingles raced up Gwen's arm, and instantly she knew she'd made a mistake. She'd told herself to keep her distance. Now, all she wanted to do was get closer still. Gwen released his grip, attempting to steady herself on wobbly knees. If merely shaking hands had this much effect, she'd hate to see the pool of putty she'd be in if he'd dared to kiss her.

"Have you eaten anything since lunch?" he asked with concern.

Gwen pulled herself together, realizing she must have suddenly paled. "I had some wine and cheese back at the inn."

"Havarti?" he asked, with uncanny insight.

"How did you…?"

He repressed a grin, pointing to the back of her head. Gwen ran panicked fingers through her hair, finding a nice little chunk of cheese caught up in her curls.

She stared at him, mortified. "I'm so embarrassed," she began.

"Don't be," he offered kindly. "I get Camembert in mine all the time."

She scanned his face for the hint of a smile but couldn't detect one beneath his deadpan.

"This time, I know you're teasing," she said, and the moment between them lightened.

Small lines tugged at the corners of his mouth as blue eyes crinkled. "Something tells me you're getting to know me too well." His gaze held a hint of longing mixed with caution. "Wine and cheese isn't much of a dinner. I know a place with great steaks, if you'd like to join me?"

Gwen knew she was wrong to say yes. Everything inside her screamed *caution, slippery roads ahead.* But all Gwen wanted to do was get in that spectacular sports car and drive.

"I'd love to," she said, accepting his invitation.


Dan led them down a side street to an elegant outdoor restaurant set a few blocks from the plaza. The shaded pathway to its entrance bypassed the abutting Loretto Chapel, a notable nineteenth-century structure in Gothic Revival style, complete with buttresses and spires.

"Have you been in there?" Dan asked as they strolled by the wind art adorning the chapel's lawn.

Gwen admired the huge hands of the whimsical brass structures cupping and turning in the breeze as the sun sank low. "Not yet."

Her view panned to a fanciful wood carving of a man guarding the chapel door.

"Saint Joseph," Dan said, indicating the statue. "I'll tell you the story over dinner. You do believe in miracles?" He was smiling at her in a playful way.

A shiver shimmied down Gwen's spine, as she thought it was nothing short of miraculous that she was here, right now, with him. Dan Holbrook was not just a feast for the eyes, he was funny and kind and apparently enjoying her company. Plus, he made her feel beautiful. Not just because he'd said it. It was in the way he looked at her, all the time.

"I'll keep an open mind," she said, smiling back at him.

Dan shoved his hand in his pocket to prevent himself from reaching out and taking hers. In some ways, it would have seemed natural as he led her toward the maître d. In others, it was completely absurd! Dan heaved a sigh, grateful good sense had prevailed.

"Are you all right?" she asked, chocolate-brown eyes imploring.

"Just taking in the evening," he said, thankful there was no wait for a table.

He ordered them filet mignon with a mushroom, red pepper, and sherry reduction, Caesar salads to start, and a choice bottle of Chilean red wine. Dan didn't want to mess this up. Gwen's dinner had to be perfect. He'd slipped the maître d an unseen tip to ensure it. He'd also told Gwen upfront that the meal was on him. He'd seen the way her brow had knitted slightly as she'd surveyed the menu prices. Dan wasn't sure what sort of money trouble she was in, but he could bet her budget didn't include places like this one.

"The service is fabulous here," Gwen said as her water glass magically refilled.

Dan had the impression Gwen wasn't used to men treating her right. He was glad to be able to change that, to show her that not all men were schmucks, maybe just the ones she'd previously run into. "Wait until you taste the food."

She smiled sweetly over the rim of her wineglass. "This carménère is delicious. I'm so glad I got to try it."

"Should go well with the steak," Dan said, hoping he'd scored a point. For the life of him, he wanted to impress this woman. She looked prettier than ever, sitting there relaxed in the candle's glow. He compared her now to how she'd appeared yesterday afternoon in the gallery, anxiously combative, like if he didn't see things her way, there'd be hell to pay. He probably liked this Gwen better. Though the truth of the matter was Dan didn't really mind the other one much at all. He could see a man getting used to a balanced measure of them both.

Dan took a sip of wine, knowing he was letting his emotions get the best of him. That was a dangerous mountain to climb when he understood what was on the other side: a clean downhill slide where his heart would take a tumble. Elena had been quite detailed in enumerating his faults.

A crescent moon rose as a smattering of stars poured onto the canvas of the night sky above them. Their salads arrived, artfully served and in a timely fashion.

"So, are you going to tell me the story?" she asked eagerly.

Dan was happy for the chance to take his mind off his gloomy thoughts. "Ah yes, the story of Loretto Chapel," he said, setting down his glass. He leaned forward on his elbows and lowered his voice. "And its mysterious spiral staircase."

"Staircase?" she asked with surprise.

"Legend has it the staircase in Loretto Chapel arrived as a miracle. Some to this day may dispute it, but many others do not."

"Go on," she pressed, intrigued.

"Rumor holds that when the chapel was completed in the eighteen hundreds, the dear nuns who lived there noted there was no staircase to get them to the choir loft on the upper level."

"Oh my!"

"So they prayed for nine days for a miracle. On the tenth day, an unknown carpenter appeared and offered to complete the task. He built the freestanding staircase all by himself without using glue, nails, or any central support. Then, as soon as he was done, the stranger disappeared just as mysteriously as he'd arrived, without ever having identified himself or demanding any payment. The good sisters of Loretto naturally took this as a miracle, and the man to have been Saint Joseph himself. The proof I believe lies in the number of steps of the freestanding structure, made of a wood not even found in this region."

"Well?" she asked, her eyes twinkling.

"Thirty-three. The age of Jesus Christ."

Gwen leaned back in her chair with a delighted laugh. "That's wonderful! What a fantastic story."

"It's not a story," he said with mock defensiveness. "It's a miracle." The corners of his mouth twitched slightly, and Gwen could tell he was repressing a smile. She was finally starting to read him, and for a girl who didn't like to read, that said a lot.

Gwen cocked an eyebrow and shot him an impish smile. "Do you believe in miracles, Dan?"

He captured her with his gaze, stilling her heart for a fraction of a second. "Let's just say I believe most things in life can be rationally explained."

"Most things don't mean all," she bantered lightly.

He raised his glass to hers as their salad plates were cleared and the entrées arrived. "You've got me there."

Everything smelled delicious. Gwen couldn't wait to dig in. She hadn't realized how hungry she'd gotten subsisting on complimentary inn food these past few days.

"How's your filet?" he asked as she took a heavenly bite that literally melted in her mouth. "Cooked all right?"

He was incredibly handsome in the soft light, flames from the outdoor fire caressing the solid lines of his face.

"Perfect. Everything's just perfect. I couldn't have had a better night."

"I'm glad," he said with a grin. "That just leaves tomorrow."

"What do you mean?"

"You've got a bit of time to kill while the shipment comes in. Got any plans?"

"I thought I'd take in an art museum or two."

"That sounds great. I've been considering taking the day off myself."

Gwen set down her fork. "Are you…asking me on a date?"

"You mean unlike this one," he deadpanned.

She gasped with surprise. "This was a date?"

"It could be if you wanted it to."

Gwen's heart went fluttering in all sorts of wild directions. Why on earth was he doing this? Surely there was no sense in it. She'd be gone by the week's end. "I'm not so sure that's a good idea."

"Which one?"

"This a date… Tomorrow. I…I don't know." And she didn't, she really didn't. She was feeling all jumbled up inside, like she'd desperately wanted something and now didn't know what to do once she'd gotten it.

"How about if we just call it an appointment, then? An arrangement between associates to go and see some art.

Besides," he added temptingly, "I know who serves the best chile rellenos in town."

It was patently unfair of him to play the food card. Gwen absolutely adored chile rellenos, almost as much as she was starting to adore this man. "It's a deal," she said, smiling broadly.

Dan walked Gwen back to the inn, night sounds singing around them. He'd really jumped in headlong with this one, but Dan couldn't completely blame himself. With her lovely looks and warm and charming personality, Gwen had led him right to it. He'd been having such a good time with her at dinner, he couldn't bear having the evening end. The only remedy for that was to suggest seeing her tomorrow. He didn't have much going on at the gallery, and what was left to do Megan could take care of.

Dan stole a glimpse of Gwen strolling beside him in the moonlight and wished for a moment that things weren't transitory. But they were, and he'd need to remain aware of that. Just because they'd planned to spend the day together didn't mean they'd have to become any more involved than they already were. He liked Gwen, dammit. She was sensitive and sweet, and he felt good when he was around her. Dan hadn't felt this good about himself in a very long while. He decided it was time.

They got to the exterior patio door of Gwen's private suite, and she opened her purse to withdraw the key, her cheeks still aflame.

"I had a really great time tonight," she said, beaming up at him and feeling very much as if it had been a date.

"Me too," he said, stepping a fraction of an inch closer. Sea-blue eyes washed over her, threatening to pull her under. And boy, did she want to get swept away. "I'm glad you agreed to see me tomorrow, even if it's just an arrangement."

Gwen sensed Dan could rearrange her heart every which way, if she wasn't careful. "I'm glad I'm seeing you too," she said, feeling the warmth in her cheeks.

"Ten o'clock work for you?" he asked, his tone growing gravelly.

"Uh-huh," she uttered, mesmerized by his gaze.

He moved nearer now, his mouth just inches away. "I'll be damned if I don't want to kiss you," he said, his voice a husky rasp.

And she'd be damned if she didn't want him to. "Dan…" she said, tilting up her chin and closing her eyes.

"But I won't," he said, snapping her back to attention, eyes open. "Not now. Not here. Not like this…"

She started to speak as he brought his fingers to her lips. "If ever I've seen a woman who deserves to be kissed well, it's you. But the timing has got to be right. You have to be sure." He cast a cursory glance at her wedding band and backed away. "I need to be sure. Something tells me we've both gone down a path neither of us wants to travel again."

Gwen's heart sank as her face burned hot. He was right, and she knew it. Neither of them could risk foolishly giving themselves away. It was only a kiss, but a kiss was often the beginning. She was old enough to know that, and Dan clearly was too.

Gwen couldn't guess who'd broken Dan's heart, but he'd obviously been hurt just as much as she had.

"Good night, Gwen," he said, shadows haunting his face.

She watched him turn and walk away, loneliness settling inside her like a large, heavy weight Gwen feared she'd never shake.

She let herself into her empty room and cried softly in the darkness, moonlight weeping in through slanted blinds. If only she'd found a man like Dan ten years ago, maybe neither of them would have had to live through these vestiges of pain. But the past was long ago and should be forgotten, Gwen thought, twisting the ring on her finger.

Perhaps meeting Dan now was a good thing, the right thing for them both. Maybe they were meant to be stepping stones, each of them strategically placed to help the other on to a better life. They could be friends, confidants even, during her short stay in Santa Fe. Maybe they'd each give the other someone to lean on, somebody who really understood, for the first time in a long time. That didn't mean they'd have to start falling in love.

Gwen sucked in a breath, praying it wasn't already too late. By the way her heart hammered against her chest, she wasn't sure.

# Chapter Four

Gwen and Dan strolled toward the main plaza, stopping first at the New Mexico Museum of Art, a fortress-like structure made of adobe, of course. Gwen tried to stop Dan when he started to pay her entrance fee, but he was too quick on the draw. "It's the least I can do," he said with a smile. "We locals get in at a discount." He shot her a wink, causing the tiniest fluttering in her tummy.

"You're being really good to me," she said. "Do all of Holbrook and Holstein's artists get this VIP treatment?"

He leveled her a look as if he were considering it.

"Nope," he said, leading her into a courtyard opening up to a brilliant blue sky.

They passed in through another door and into the first-floor gallery. "This is spectacular!" she said, taking in wall after wall of New Mexican and Native American art.

"There are a couple of pieces in particular I think you'd like to see," he said, leading her around the corner.

Gwen came face-to-face with her first authentic Georgia O'Keeffe, *Blue River*, and it took her breath away. "It's stunning," she told Dan, absorbing this wildly vibrant rendering of the Chama River snaking through the New Mexico hills.

Dan's eyes twinkled with delight. "There's more," he said, steering her into the next room, where more famous pieces awaited, including a glorious portrayal of the Cerro Pedernal, the unique flat-topped mesa favored by O'Keeffe in her desert landscape series. "She painted this one during her time at Ghost Ranch, northwest of the city here. She called it 'my mountain,' stating God had granted her authority to claim it were she to paint it often enough."

Gwen laughed from the tale and the sheer joy of the moment. She felt so in her element here, among these great works with this great man. "It's almost intimidating to see her art," she admitted honestly. "It was so ahead of its time, revolutionary. It's inspiring yet overwhelming at once."

"I believe each artist has her own special gifts to offer," Dan said, meeting her eyes as her heart skipped a beat. Dan brought his palm to her cheek and cupped it gently. She felt faint from his touch. "You're very talented, Gwen. I've seen your work, and I trust it will sell."

"I hope you're right," she said breathlessly.

"Have faith," he said, his gaze diving into her. "I do. I have faith in your work, in you."

Dan withdrew his hand, and Gwen's pulse galloped into overdrive. She tried to move forward but felt light-headed. "I think I need to eat something," she said.

"I've got just the ticket for that," he said with a grin.

They settled on a shady park bench in the main plaza, Dan having purchased a couple of bottles of water and two huge plates from a vendor cart. The chile rellenos were enormous, stuffed with melted cheese and deep fried in a light batter. "This is like biting into a slice of heaven," Gwen said, savoring the healthy heat provided by the peppers.

"Try it with a bit of fresh-made salsa," Dan said, passing over a small plastic cup. "I'll warn you, it's got a kick."

Gwen thrilled at the thought her food could get any spicier than it already was. She was a daredevil when it came to tastes. She eagerly accepted the salsa and dumped it on her chilies.

"Whoa! Not so much," he tried to warn, but it was too late. The golden fried peppers were already swimming in a sea of red. Dan handed over some water. "You'd better take this."

"I'll be all right," she insisted, picking up her plastic fork and taking a sizable bite. Fire scorched her tongue as flames leapt up her nasal passages and spiked down her throat. "Argh!" she cried, grasping desperately for the water as tears sprang from her eyes. She uncapped the bottle and chugged half of it down while Dan released a belly laugh. "What's so funny?" she asked, dabbing at her streaming face with paper napkins.

"Like things hot, do you?" he said, repressing a grin.

She elbowed him in a playful way. "Be nice."

"I am nice," he said sincerely. "Very nice, in fact. Some even say I'm the most eligible bachelor in the Southwest."

"I'll bet that's true," she said, taking another swallow of water. "And I know why you're still a bachelor too."

He raised his brow at her, questioning.

"You've killed off all your interested admirers with inordinate amounts of hot sauce!"

Dan boomed another laugh, then met her gaze. "So, you're an interested admirer, now? I thought we agreed to be just friends?" And they had too. Dan had brought it up as soon as he'd seen her. They hadn't even cleared the inn's parking lot before he'd told her what a mistake he'd made last night and apologized for intimating anything beyond friendship was possible. Gwen had absorbed his apology with a mixture of understanding and regret. Naturally, she told him, she felt exactly the same.

"I only hope you find a woman someday who's strong enough to take it," she teased.

"That would be a catch worth hanging on to," he agreed, enjoying his own lunch. "I grow my own jalapeños, you know."

"Do you?" she asked with surprise. "Where?"

"Why, out on Paradise Ranch."

"Paradise?" she queried. "That sounds lovely."

"It's nice enough," he said. "Nice and peaceful."

"Where is it exactly?"

"Not far outside of town, up a ways on Highway Eighty-four."

"Do you spend most of your time there?"

"As much as I can manage."

"Is it a family place?" she asked innocently.

Dan's eyes clouded over like the ocean before a storm. "I'm not much on family these days. It's just me and Nancy, really, and she keeps a place in the city."

"I'm sorry, Dan. I didn't know. Your parents... Have they been gone long?"

"Cancer took my mom several years ago. My dad set out on his own way before. Never really heard much from or about him after that." The fine creases around his mouth hardened, resisting the bitter memory. Gwen's heart ached for him.

"I know what that's like," she said softly. "My dad ran out on us too."

He turned toward her, emotion shadowing his face. "I'm sorry to hear that. That's a hard thing to have happened to you, you and Marian both. How's your mom holding up?"

Gwen hung her head, the admission cutting to her core. "She's not doing well. She doesn't even know who we are half the time. Marian and I had to put her in a home because she'd started wandering."

Dan looked distant a moment, his thoughts roaming. "That's really rough," he said after a while. "That must take a lot of strength to deal with."

She met his calm and comforting gaze. How could he be so impossibly easy to talk to when the topic was so unbelievably hard? "I'm getting stronger every day," she said, hoping that saying so would make it true.

Dan shot her a melancholy smile. "I once knew someone who used that expression a lot."

"Yeah?"

"My baby sister, Jocelyn" he said, looking away.

"You didn't... lose her too?" Gwen asked with concern.

Dan turned back to her, his expression worn. The air hung heavy between them while he seemed to weigh a decision.

"I didn't mean to pry."

"I brought it up, not you," he said with a gentle smile. "And yes, we lost her. Funny thing is, I still miss her every day."

A swell of sorrow overtook her as she studied this kind, compassionate man. "I'm sorry."

"Didn't mean to bring the conversation down."

"It's not down. We were just talking." She felt her face flush at the admission. "I like talking to you."

He stroked his chin and scrutinized her. "Is that a fact?"

It most certainly was. So much of a fact that if he didn't stop looking at her in that heart-pounding way, Gwen didn't trust what might come out of her mouth next.

"Are you up for one more stop?" he asked, blue eyes brightening.

Gwen nodded, still unable to unstick her tongue from the roof of her mouth.

"That's good," he said, mildly nudging her plate. "Better fuel up on the hot stuff to keep you going."

She wrinkled her nose, and the moment between them lightened. "You really are trying to kill me, aren't you?" she said with a laugh.

"Not on your life," he replied with a wink. "I like my up-and-coming artists alive and well."

Dan sat beside Gwen on the boxy, rectangular bench, the biographic film on Georgia O'Keeffe's life nearly over. The video was as much about O'Keeffe and her work that hung here as it was about the man who'd had the greatest influence on her. Photographer Alfred Stieglitz was not only the patron who sponsored her first art show in New York, he'd become her friend and confidant, and eventually her lover, capturing many provocative images of O'Keeffe with his camera. Dan rested his hand on the bench beside him, inadvertently brushing the edge of Gwen's. His fingers ached to extend and take hold of hers. He drummed the ceramic bench beneath him to keep them from acting out on their own.

As the credits rolled and the house lights came up, Gwen gave him a soft smile. "What a beautiful story," she said. "I had no idea about O'Keeffe and Stieglitz and how they'd influenced each other. It's interesting how he began as her benefactor, and then the two of them fell in love."

"He believed in her," Dan said, holding her gaze. She colored lightly around her cheekbones, and Dan found himself wanting to reach up and touch her again as he had in the larger museum.

She stood suddenly, like she'd read his mind. "He was a good bit older, it seems," Gwen said as they cleared the room with the rest of the crowd.

"Perhaps a little," Dan agreed. "But sometimes age doesn't matter."

"Maybe not." She colored a shade deeper. "They understood each other. That's what counts."

Dan held back the door, and they stepped into the sunshine. "Probably helps that they started as friends."

She stopped on the sidewalk and looked up at him, dark eyes brimming with affection. "I've had the best day today," she said, smiling sweetly.

Dan hoped he was reading her right and that she liked him as much as he did her. So what if she was just here for a few days? When Dan was around her, he felt strong and capable, like there was no mountain too high for him to climb. "I have too," he said, smiling back. "I hate the thought I have to head back."

"To the gallery?" she questioned.

Dan's cell buzzed, and he checked it briefly with a frown.

"There are some things I need to look into before closing," he said, tucking his phone away. "Can I see you back to the inn?"

"Thanks, but I think I'll stay in town a little longer, look around at a few of the shops."

"There's another museum," he offered. "That is, unless you're arted out."

"I think I'm done for the day. I really appreciate you showing me around. The chile rellenos were the best."

He wanted to ask her to dinner but felt he shouldn't push it. Dan didn't want to overwhelm her, despite the fact that he was starting to feel he could never get enough of Gwen.

"I'll be working tomorrow during the day as well. I'll want to be sure all's going smoothly with a special shipment coming in. But I'll be free by dinnertime. How about you?"

She smiled at him brightly. "I haven't made plans."

"How does pizza with a spectacular mountain view sound?"

"Totally awesome," she said with a grin.

"Pick you up about eight fifteen?"

"Sounds super, Dan. Thank you."

"Will you be okay for dinner tonight?"

"Oh yes, fine. I'm still stuffed from lunch. I'll probably just fix myself a small cheese plate."

"Watch out for that Havarti," he said, repressing a smile. "I've heard it's very aggressive."

When Gwen laughed, the sound resonated like music to his soul. "That it is," she agreed. "I'll be sure to take care."

Gwen spent the rest of the afternoon meandering through the small shops of Santa Fe. Just for fun, she tried on a Stetson and a pair of turquoise-and-white cowgirl boots at the Wild West Boutique just east of the plaza. Examining her reflection in the mirror, Gwen couldn't help but grin. Who was this wholesome and happy-looking woman? Could it possibly be her? Gwen found herself wondering what Dan would think of the getup, deciding he'd probably like it. There didn't appear to be much about her he didn't like. It was such an unusual juxtaposition relative to how she'd felt with Robert. With Robert, she'd felt under a microscope, as if everything she did was scrutinized, and generally not in a very flattering way.

She returned the hat to the rack, running her fingers through her curls. Dan had even seemed to enjoy her unintended tango with Havarti! Gwen tried to imagine how Robert might have reacted. He likely would have called her stupid or inept for not having checked herself better before leaving the inn. Robert didn't appreciate being embarrassed, and she apparently did plenty to embarrass him in front of his wealthy, film-set friends. She was either too quiet or too loud, either clamming up like an idiot with nothing too interesting to say or running her mouth off for no good reason about things nobody else in the world would be concerned with. A fund-raiser for the children's hospital? How utterly gauche of Gwen to bring it up. It was like she expected them to donate just because they could. That was no sort of social conversation starter!

Gwen kicked off the cowgirl boots, wishing she'd given Robert a swift kick in the pants as he was leaving. The fact that she hadn't showed she actually possessed the better part of self-control when it was necessary. For one thing, she hadn't wanted to give Robert the satisfaction of knowing how much he'd both outraged and hurt her. That was her little secret.

Gwen set the boots back on the shelf, her gaze grazing the gold wedding band. During their first year of marriage, she'd wondered so many times why Robert had taken the trouble to give it to her. His were hollow vows, eked out in the dim light of a small church on a moss-covered lane. Gwen's heart had brimmed with joy that day, not having any inkling of what was coming. Less than six months down the road, he was ringing up old girlfriends and partying until dawn with the movie crew. It had taken Gwen a while to confess to her sister what was really going on, and Marian had been furious. Tom wasn't perfect by any stretch, but at least he had his weakness to offer up as an excuse. Robert, on the other hand, was just plain mean, evil in a way no man had a right to be with his brand-new wife.

Gwen steadied her chin, thinking it was good to know that not all men were wicked. Some, in fact, were thoughtful and kind, and actually took time to listen. Gwen's heart fluttered, recalling Dan's gentle touch in the art museum. It wasn't just the heat of his skin that had sent her pulse racing. There'd been a telling warmth in his eyes as well. And when he said he had faith in her, Gwen had absolutely believed it. Gwen was glad she'd have some downtime this evening. She needed the breather to sort through her thoughts. Despite what they both officially claimed, seeing Dan was feeling more and more like dating. While chile rellenos in the plaza spelled casual, dinner with a view seemed cocktail level at least.

Gwen picked the boots up anew, considering how much fun it would be to wear them. Then again, money was tight, and she couldn't afford to spend on luxuries when she'd come to raise funds for her and her sister's real-time needs. "Maybe one day," she told the boots, as if they could hear her.

Gwen left the boutique, wondering if that day would ever come. How amazing it would be not to spend every waking hour concerned about money. In that moment, Gwen realized she'd never really aspired to being rich. All she wanted to do was feel comfortable, as if she at minimum knew where her next meal was coming from. If she was able to paint and sell her art on top of that, she'd find herself in some sort of incredible nirvana she'd been afraid to imagine up until now.

Gwen's imagination started to run away with her as she envisioned a handsome, blue-eyed rancher riding up on his horse. Dan could take her to paradise, all right. There and back again several times over, Gwen was sure. She blushed brilliantly at the thought of Dan pulling her close, as she was growing desperate for him to do. Gwen moistened her suddenly dry lips as the setting sun bore down on her. Could she trust him enough to give up everything? To become involved on a level so personal? A distant wind blew, rippling her flirty sundress in the breeze.

Gwen hustled back to the inn, sheer fabric hugging her thighs. Her breasts and belly warmed at the thought of seeing him, and Gwen understood this was no longer a Caribbean swell she was fighting. It was a tidal wave.

# Chapter Five

Dan made small talk with the two bronzed women from Austin. The sisters were here on holiday with a few other girlfriends and staying at one of the large establishments offering full spa services. They'd been quick to let Dan know their oil-industry husbands had provided them with shopping money and that they were interested in picking up art.

"Holbrook and Holstein's expecting a new acquisition later this week, in fact," he told them. "Promising new artist with a very keen eye. Gwendolyn Marsh. Maybe you've heard of her?"

Dan's gaze flitted to the front window, surprised to think he'd just seen her walk by. He was letting his imagination get the better of him, believing any blonde bopping down the street might be Gwen.

The taller one clapped her hands together with glee. Silver bangles dangled from slim wrists. "Wonderful! What sort of work does she do?"

"Seascapes and bits of ocean wildlife. She gives them a very interesting and unique treatment in oils."

"I adore anything oil," she said, rolling her eyes at her sister, who was busy retouching her lipstick. She smacked thin lips together, then checked her image in a compact purse mirror.

"Um-hmm," she agreed. "Absolutely. Maybe you'll pick up something for Shangri-La?"

"Vacation home on the Gulf Coast," the first one said to Dan by way of explanation.

"I think these might be well suited to a place like that. I hope you'll drop back by?"

"Of course we will," the shorter one said, suddenly taking charge. Her sister raised both eyebrows. "Well, I wouldn't want you to pass up the opportunity. You heard what he said; it might be perfect for you. Besides, you don't know how many others he's advised to stop in."

Both shot Dan inquiring, green-eyed glances. "I have to admit I've been spreading the word," he said pleasantly.

"That settles it, then," the shorter one said.

"Emily's right, I am intrigued. When will the new work be available to view?"

"The day after tomorrow. We open at ten."

"Delightful!" the taller woman said. "My name's Victoria, by the way," she said, offering Dan her hand. "Victoria Kent."

"Dan Holbrook," he said, with a short, businesslike handshake.

"Holbrook as in Holbrook and Holstein?" Emily inquired.

"One and the same," Dan said with a pleasant smile. "Although the real brains behind the operation belongs to my sister, Nancy."

"I can see where the muscle comes in," Emily added with an admiring gaze.

Dan thought he saw Gwen pass by again.

"Excuse me just one second," he said, striding to the door and peering outside. A figure in a flouncy skirt and highly stylized boots slipped around the corner.

"Everything all right?" Victoria called from the gallery's center.

"Just thought I recognized someone," Dan said, wondering if he was losing his mind. "I hope to see you both back here on Friday."

"We wouldn't miss it for the world, would we, Victoria?" Emily said in a tone that was a tad too flirty.

"Not for the world," Victoria agreed with a bright smile.

Gwen scurried around the corner, then stopped to catch her breath. Was she out of her mind? She must have strolled past Holbrook and Holstein's array of windows a half dozen times, just hoping to catch sight of him. And then, when she had, he'd been caught up in conversation with two gorgeous women!

"Excuse me, honey," the first one said, nearly running over her.

Gwen scooted out of the way as the pair closed in. The shorter one pointed to Gwen's feet, then shot Gwen an appreciative look. "Radical boots!" she said, strolling by. She linked arms with the other one, and the two of them strode off, sharing private jokes and laughter, their pencil-thin legs gleaming in the sunlight.

Gwen felt her face burn hot and ducked into a nearby gallery to cool off. So okay, she'd had a weak moment. Not long after she'd opted not to buy these boots, she'd decided she had to. How often did she treat herself anyway? The answer was never. Gwen had spent her whole life on a financial tightrope of one sort or another. Growing up, she'd felt guilty about the sacrifices her single mother constantly made; then in marriage, she'd been burdened with Robert's unending scrutiny. After the divorce, she'd scarcely had two coins to rub together and had a debt crisis to recover from besides. She wasn't about to indulge in extravagances. But the truth was Gwen was tired, flat-out exhausted from the merciless monetary restraint. She wanted one thing, just one little thing, that she could buy and claim as hers without feeling as if she'd have to head straight to church afterwards.

Feeling emboldened by the wine-and-cheese hour, she'd pranced right back to the Wild West Boutique and extracted her charge card. It had been a glorious moment, preceded by heady anticipation. Gwen was about to do something wonderful for herself and not get caught! Or so she hoped. Just to ensure her moral turpitude wouldn't count against her, Gwen had dropped by Loretto Chapel on the way back to the inn. Comforted by Catholic memorabilia, fresh flowers, and dripping rosaries, she'd immediately felt her sin absolved. There she was in the presence of the miraculous staircase, for heaven's sake! How could the Mighty Savior give a fiddle about fancy boots when there were such acts of grandeur to contemplate?

Gwen ducked behind an indoor sculpture as a man matching Dan's description passed by on the street. She'd presumably come to check out her future competitors on Canyon Road and spend a leisurely day browsing the art. Instead, she'd engaged in clandestine observations of her generous benefactor. The fact that Dan was also handsome, funny, and kind only lent power to his voracious, voodoo-like hold on her. Gwen had to get a grip!

"Can I help you with something?" a well-dressed woman inquired, staring down at her crouched form near the floor.

"Just dropped an earring!" Gwen lied, straightening quickly.

"There, you see," she said, holding up nothing in her hand but keeping her grip closed so the woman couldn't tell. "Found it!"

Then, before the woman could ask her anything more, like was she in need of directions to the loony bin, Gwen shuffled out the door.

Dan's cell buzzed anew, sparking his irritation. Sooner or later, he'd have to deal with this, but it wouldn't be tonight. Tonight, he planned to be all Gwen's. It was odd how he'd believed he'd seen her walking by. He supposed, as an artist, it would be natural for her to peruse the other galleries on Canyon Road. Yet, if that had been her, why hadn't she dropped in to say hello? And why couldn't he knock that nagging feeling that he hadn't simply glimpsed her once, he'd seen her skirt by at least half a dozen times?

Dan shook his head, feeling like a naive young kid, daydreaming of his crush at every turn. Perspiration built at Dan's brow and warmed the nape of his neck. He adjusted his open collar, which suddenly felt too tight. Things were creeping up on him. Gwen was starting to mean more to him than he'd originally planned. He surveyed the blinking red light on his BlackBerry, then slid open a desk drawer and tucked the offending object inside. Whatever the emergency was this time, it would have to wait.

# Chapter Six

Gwen sat across the table from Dan, who looked more delectable than anything on the menu. He was dressed in a casual white shirt and jeans, their cut fitting nicely on his tall, toned frame. "What looks good to you?" he asked.

"Everything," she said, making an attempt to study the choices. "What do you recommend?"

"The Californian is good."

"All veggies?" Gwen asked with surprise.

"What? I'm allowed to eat healthy."

And boy, didn't he have the body to show for it. "That's fine. I love portabella mushrooms and sundried tomatoes."

"That was easy," he said, setting their menus aside. "Would you like me to order the wine?"

"I'd love for you to order the wine. I'm still learning my way around it. Good wine, I mean. I know all about Two Buck Charlie!"

Dan spouted a laugh. "Oh yes, I've heard about that one. Rare vintage, is it?"

"It's not bad, honestly. But it's not nearly as good as the wines you pick out."

"Well, thank you." He folded his arms across his broad chest and leaned back in his chair, satisfied. "I aim to please."

In a flash, wild images of all the ways in which Dan might please Gwen raced through her mind. She lifted the small Specialty Drinks menu card to fan her blazing face.

"Think we might ask for some water?" she squeaked.

Dan leaned forward with concern. "You feeling all right?"

"Just had a long day walking around town. Probably dehydrated."

"You weren't up on Canyon Road by any chance?"

"Canyon Road?" she repeated like an idiotic parrot.

"You know, up my way. Where all the galleries are?"

Gwen crossed one calf over the other, the leather of her boots squealing.

Dan peeked under the table. "Well, I'll be! I could have sworn I…"

"Canyon Road! Why yes, yes, actually, I was. I was up there, over that way, earlier this afternoon, I believe?"

Dan slowly cocked an eyebrow. "Don't you think you're neglecting to say something?" Gwen swallowed hard. This was it. She'd been caught red-handed, stalking a man who wasn't even her boyfriend! "Like where you got those dynamite boots?" he continued.

Gwen blinked and sucked in a breath, fresh air cleansing like an absolution.

"The boots! Oh yes! I got them at the Wild West Boutique."

Dan let loose a high, shrill whistle. "Upscale place."

"Aren't they a kick?"

"They're great, Gwen. They really suit you. Did you get them today?"

"Yesterday, when I was shopping around after the museums."

"Well, it's good to see you didn't let your afternoon go to waste," he said with a smile.

"Oh, I didn't. I absolutely didn't! I saw Loretto Chapel, too!"

"So, what did you think? About the staircase?"

"I thought it was awesome. Really and truly. Whether or not you believe in the miracle, it's certainly something to see."

Nope, what was something to see sat right across from him. Gwen was gorgeous in that sexy peasant top, long, lacy earrings dangling against the inviting line of her neck. Dan studied her expression, noting she appeared happy and carefree. The way her deep brown eyes caught the soft light was nothing short of amazing. The sun set beyond them, casting long shadows across the mountains surrounding Santa Fe

"It's beautiful up here," she said, looking around. "You were right about the view."

"I like what I'm looking at," he said, diving into her with his eyes. Color dusted her cheekbones as the wine steward arrived with their selection. Dan tasted and accepted the bottle, then handed Gwen her poured glass.

"What do we drink to?" she asked.

"How about to fortune?"

"To good fortune for the two of us," she said, clinking his glass.

In that instant, Dan knew he was doomed. Gwen was beautiful in the sunset, soft gold curls framing her face. And she wasn't just a looker, either. Gwen was sweet and kind and just the kind of woman he could trust with his secrets. Dan had surprised himself in the plaza when he'd told her about his dad. That was a subject Dan didn't like to talk about, and one which he never brought up. There were things beyond that he longed to tell her. Things that were very personal and he'd shared with few other people. Would she reject him if he told her the truth? His track record with other women in that regard hadn't been exactly stellar.

"Why Dan Holbrook, I thought that was you."

Gwen watched the color drain from Dan's face as the beautiful brunette approached.

"Elena?" Dan said, barely choking out the word.

Elena positioned her sunglasses on top of her head, revealing spectacular green eyes. "You're a hard man to track down."

"I didn't know you were looking," Dan said, tension hedging his voice.

"Maybe that's because you don't pick up your phone."

Dan turned toward Gwen, his complexion flushed. "Oh Gwen, I'm sorry. This is Elena—"

"Caldova," the woman cut in, extending a suntanned arm in Gwen's direction. "The ex."

Gwen swallowed hard past the lump in her throat and shook Elena's hand. "Gwendolyn Marsh. Nice to meet you."

Elena studied Gwen's face, then cast a judgmental glance at her bright turquoise cowgirl boots. "And you are...?"

"She's a client, Elena. Not that it's any business of yours."

Gwen's heart sank in her chest that she'd been introduced this way. But of course, what would she expect?

Elena perused the expensive bottle of wine on the table. "Looks like business is good."

"It was better just a few moments ago," Dan said, surprising Gwen with his acidic tone. He pushed back his chair and stood in a brusque fashion. "If you'll excuse me a minute," he told Gwen, laying aside his napkin.

"Of course," she said, her gut on fire.


"All right, Elena," Dan said, leveling her a hard look. "What's this all about?"

"The two of us, Dan. You and me. What else?"

"You know as well as I do that the two of us are done."

"You didn't think so last month in Albuquerque."

"I was wrong."

"That's not what you said back at my apartment," she said with a smirk.

"Running into you at the airport couldn't be helped. Agreeing to have drinks with you afterwards was a big mistake." Dan had kicked himself a million times since. He'd scarcely put Nancy on the plane when he'd felt that familiar tug at his elbow. There Elena had stood, looking lovelier than ever but with a piteous pout on her lips. She'd just lost her cousin to cancer and had flown back from the funeral. There were so many memories, and she was so broken up. If only she could talk to an old friend, just for a while. Surely they were adult enough to still be friends?

"Dan, I have something to tell you," she said, a moist sheen coating her eyes.

"Oh no you don't, Elena. You're not pulling that on me this time. I've had more than enough of your—"

"It's important," she said, stopping him mid-rant.

"Important, Elena? What is it this time? Another dead relative?"

He'd learned later through a mutual acquaintance that Elena's story had been a half-truth. Her cousin hadn't died at all. She'd merely been recovering from appendicitis.

"That was low, Dan. Even for you."

"No, what's low, Elena, is you showing up here. You're the one who walked out on me, as I recall. And in your own words, with plenty of good reason."

"You really haven't changed a bit," she said, setting her jaw.

"Probably not," Dan agreed. "Now, if you'll excuse me, I have a dinner date to return to."

"I thought she was a business colleague?"

"Nothing in my life concerns you anymore," he said, turning away. "Or vice versa."

"Don't be so sure," she said, her voice cracking.

Dan turned slowly to face her. "What's that supposed to mean?"

By the time Dan returned to their table, the pizza had been sitting there for ten minutes.

"I'm sorry, Gwen. Sorry you had to see that."

"I didn't know you'd been married before. Of course, why would I?" she said, her world still reeling around her.

"Not married. Never was. But Elena and I were engaged." He had an odd look about him, as if he were feeling quite unwell.

"Is everything all right?" Gwen asked with concern.

Dan furrowed his brow in concentration, then downed a sip of wine as if he hadn't heard her.

Gwen met his eyes, feeling the heat in her own. "Maybe we should go."

"No. No way. Absolutely not," he said, regaining composure. "I apologize that the evening got thrown off course this way." He glanced down at the pizza. "Bet that's stone cold by now. I'll send it back. Get us another."

"You really don't have to."

He met her eyes with a sincere gaze. "But I want to. Gwen, you don't understand how much I looked forward to this evening. I wanted us to spend time together. Still want that, even now."

Gwen wondered what the "even now" part meant but felt she shouldn't ask.

"I want to spend time with you too," she said, feeling the raw burn in her chest.

Dan's expression brightened. "Then good! Let's regroup here. Send this disgustingly healthy pizza back and order something wicked."

"You mean with fatty meats and anchovies?" Gwen bantered, trying to play things lightly.

"Anything your heart desires."

What Gwen's heart desired was that no blast from Dan's past had ever resurfaced to disturb their evening. The notion that anybody else might try to lay claim to this increasingly marvelous man secretly upset her. Given Dan's looks and impeccable taste, Gwen certainly imagined he'd been involved before. She just didn't like coming face-to-face with the evidence, particularly when it shouted upscale elegance like that. Elena was a beautiful woman, sharply sophisticated too. Gwen wasn't so sure her small-town-girl appeal could hold up under such big-city competition.

"Gwen?" Dan asked. "You do still want anchovies?"

Gwen blinked, noting their server had appeared and was waiting on her answer.

"Oh yes. Yes, please," she answered, braving a smile. "That would be fine."

All through dinner, Dan heard the echo of Elena's parting pronouncement banging about in his brain. It couldn't possibly be true. This had to be another one of Elena's convoluted ploys. But to what end? Dan steadied his intellect to focus on the problem, knowing he'd work it out eventually. There was no way in Hades he was going back to her, he thought, settling his gaze on the soft Southern beauty before him. Gwen was so warm and trusting, and things between them were just getting off the ground. He'd aimed to ask Gwen to go away with him to Taos tomorrow and was more determined than ever to make good on those intentions. Dan refused to let someone from his past throw a monkey wrench into his plans.

Especially someone as calculating as Elena. She had to be after something from Dan. The question was what?

Before Gwen was ready for the evening to be over, the waiter was clearing their dessert plates and bringing the check. They had managed to move on as if the interlude with Elena hadn't happened, but it had remained an unwelcome presence looming above them nonetheless. Why on earth would Dan's ex think to show up now? He clearly hadn't been pleased to see her and later had seemed shaken by their exchange.

Perhaps he'd simply told her to bugger off and explained he had a new life now. Yes, that had to be it, Gwen tried to reassure herself. Why else would Dan assert immediately afterwards he only wanted to spend time with her?

"I suppose tomorrow will be a busy day with the canvases coming in," Gwen said, sorry to think Dan would be tied up at the gallery again, even though that work would ultimately benefit her.

"Actually, I was just thinking the opposite. The shipment likely won't come until late in the day, and I've already asked Megan to take care of signing for it. As long as we're back by closing to double-check and unpack things, I think we'll be fine."

*As long as we're back...* "Are we going somewhere?" Gwen asked, unable to mask the hopeful anticipation in her voice.

Dan leveled her a look with those sky-blue eyes. "As long as you're taking in Santa Fe, I thought you might like to see Taos too. We can take the high road up through the mountains, then drive the low road back along the Rio Grande."

Gwen's face warmed, a billion butterflies inside her taking flight. Perhaps she'd overanalyzed Dan's encounter with Elena. That silly, overbaked, rail-thin woman clearly meant nothing to him at all. She could scarcely believe it. Was he finally going to ask her out? "Are you…?"

"Yes, Gwen," he said. "I'm asking you on a date. Not an engagement, or an arrangement, but a good, old-fashioned, day-long date." Dan's lips tugged into a smile smile so tenuous and vulnerable she hadn't thought him capable of it. "Please tell me that you'll go."

# Chapter Seven

Taos Pueblo sat on a grassy plain between sharply angled mountains. Gwen stood by the gated archway of the old cemetery, viewing the flat-topped adobe houses currently in use. "Are you sure we're allowed to go in here?" she whispered, feeling as if she were intruding on a ghost town. Though the reservation was actively inhabited, she barely saw signs of life, save the occasional stray dog shuffling by.

"We paid for the privilege," Dan whispered back. "Go on. I think I spot a tour group up ahead."

Gwen spied the referenced gaggle of tourists peering into an open doorway. They reverently followed their Native American guide through the maze of narrow pathways, taking a furtive photo here and there, careful not to use flash.

"Aren't people allowed to take pictures?" she asked him quietly.

"Sure they are," he said with a wink. "But you're supposed to pay for that privilege too." Dan motioned her around the corner, past more simple dwellings and a few vendors selling cold drinks and trinkets. "This way!"

Dan led her into an open space facing two enormous multistoried buildings. Made entirely of red clay abode, the structures stood tall against the backdrop of the mountains, individual wooden ladders leading to the upper level openings that served as doors.

"People have been living in these for more than a thousand years."

"Wow, this is amazing!"

The haunting sound of a wooden flute rippled toward them on a steady breeze. Gwen turned to see an old man playing with his eyes closed. "I thought I heard one of those playing in the plaza," she said to Dan.

"It's something to hear, especially in a place like this one."

Gwen's senses were enlivened by the melancholy melody. "It's magical, really. Almost like we've stepped back in time."

"If I were to go there, I'd certainly take you," he said holding her hand.

Gwen's heart beat like a leather drum in time to the music.

"Gwen," he continued, "I know I'm not supposed to feel this way, not with you only being in New Mexico for such a short while, but I..." He turned his gaze on hers, cascading waves shimmering in the sunshine. "I want you to know how very special it is to me that you agreed to spend this time together.

"This is probably more than you want, more than you're ready for right now, and I don't mean to push you. It's just that, Gwen. I need to be with you. Even if it's just for now and nothing more. Does that make sense?"

She looked up at this beautiful man, standing radiant in the breeze, his brow knitted with uncertainty, and her heart did a million unexpected cartwheels.

"It makes perfect sense to me," she told him. "Everything you said I agree with, Dan. What I'm saying is, I feel the same way too. I can think of nothing better than spending time with you."

He took her other hand as well and spun her toward him with a wickedly handsome grin. "That settles it, then. We'll just have to reserve the time on our calendars."

"Consider yourself penned in," she said, her soul dancing and sprinting in the wind.

Little lines tugged at the corners of his mouth as blue eyes crinkled.

"I'm relieved you didn't say penciled."

Gwen laughed with delight as he pulled her into a hug, her back pressed to his chest, her gaze facing the mountains. "Seen enough?" he asked, his breath tickling her ear. Shivers raced down her spine and shimmied to her tailbone.

"Of this view, yes," she answered breathlessly.

"Good," he said, giving her neck an affectionate nudge. "Then let's have lunch."

Gwen had to admit she was starved. Laying her heart on the line for Dan must have consumed quite a few calories. "Only if you'll do me a favor," she said coquettishly.

"Anything," he said, turning her to face him. "Anything at all."

"Order me an avocado margarita?" she asked with an impish smile.

Gwen smiled at Dan over her iced coffee and took a big bite of chocolate chip cookie. "This has been so much fun. I'm glad you suggested getting out of Santa Fe."

They'd shared a delicious lunch at a chic vegetarian place, then had taken their time tooling around the small town just south of Taos Pueblo. Quaint boutiques and outdoor eateries lined the main streets of this tiny burg tucked up in the New Mexico hills. A burgeoning ski resort in winter, it was as sleepy as a summer sunset in July, random pockets of tourists mixing in with the laid-back locals. Dan set down his coffee on the art deco tabletop of the offbeat outside café.

"Gwen," he said with a seriousness that took her aback. "I've got something I need to tell you." There was a hesitation in his voice she hadn't heard before.

Gwen felt her stomach wrench in anticipation. Whatever he was about to say couldn't be good news. She felt suddenly ill, all jittery and nauseous as if she'd consumed too much caffeine. The trouble was she'd only taken one sip.

"Remember that day in the park when I mentioned Jocelyn?"

"Your sister?" she asked, headily confused.

"That's right, my younger sister. The one who passed."

He averted her gaze and hung his head, looking deeply ashamed. Seconds ticked by so slowly Gwen could hear the clatter of each cup and saucer cleared by the busboy.

"Dan? What's going on?" she asked softly.

He stared straight at her then, blue eyes rimmed with sorrow. "I'm afraid that was my fault. All of it, my fault."

Gwen leaned forward touching the arm of this kind, caring man. While Gwen hadn't known him long, she sensed in her bones he wasn't the sort to willingly inspire any kind of family tragedy. "But, how can this be?"

"She wanted to go riding. God knows there was nothing Jocelyn loved more than riding that palomino." He almost smiled at the memory, but this time the tug at his lips was remorseful. "But my mom was plum set against it."

"Against it? But why?"

He pursed his lips a moment before continuing. "Jocelyn wasn't a regular girl. She was special, you know?"

"Like...disabled?" Gwen was floundering here and feeling as if they were wading into dangerous territory. She didn't want to offend him by guessing wrong, but she did genuinely want to understand.

"Jocelyn had a rare condition, cystic fibrosis."

"The lung disease?"

"Manageable but very serious. Most sufferers don't live beyond thirty."

He paused a moment, letting the weight of that sink in.

"My dad was of the opinion, go on, let her lead a normal life. My mom was very protective."

"What did you think?" she asked softly.

"I...agreed with my dad," he said, struggling for the words.

Gwen met his gaze with tenderness. She could see these were difficult admissions for him, perhaps even ones he'd shared with very few other people.

"Like I said, Jocelyn loved to go riding, but our mom would never let her. She was worried the activity might spur an attack."

"Did it?" Gwen asked sincerely.

"Sometimes. But Jocelyn said it was worth it. My dad said, *'Let the girl do what she wants. It's her life anyway.'*

"I used to help her tack up her horse. We'd sneak into the barn, and I'd get it all ready. There was so little I could do for her..."

"I'm sure you didn't mean her any harm."

"Of course not. She was my baby sister." Dan set his jaw, meeting her gaze. "I loved her like no brother could. She was smart, funny, irreverent..." His voice trailed off, lost in emotion.

Gwen reached out and touched his hand. "I'm sure she knew that."

"She died when she was riding, Gwen. She was practicing a jump but fell off."

"None of that was your fault!" Gwen protested, her heart brimming with sorrow for him. How could someone as good, as kind as Dan believe he'd had anything intentional to do with that?

"My mom was heartbroken. She and my dad fought about it afterwards. He rode off and left his family behind him, unable to cope with the stress."

Gwen ached for Dan having lived through this. How many years had he carried the burden of this guilt regarding circumstances that were so much beyond his control?

"You were only a teenager. You didn't want for any of that to happen. Sometimes bad things do. It's the world that we live in."

"I know," he said gravely. "Believe me, I understand it's a world that you've lived in too. Life isn't always fair, which is why I thought I should tell you."

"Tell me what?"

"The gene for cystic fibrosis is hereditary. This isn't just about Jocelyn or my dad running out. This is about the sort of man I am and what I'm from. I'm afraid it's not much of a future to offer anybody.

Dan set his jaw and turned away, emotions roiling across his rugged face. "This is one reason I've kept myself so careful about getting involved. Really, up until you, it's been two years since I've seriously cared…"

"Dan," she said, stopping him and taking his hand. "Where you're from doesn't dictate your future. Jocelyn's death was an accident. Deep inside, you must understand that. What happened to your parents was beyond your control. Many couples can't weather the loss of a child. I agree your dad was wrong to run out, but then so did mine and for no particular reason, other than growing tired of the responsibilities of raising a family."

A hardness etched across Dan's brow. "That was a terrible thing for your dad to do. It was wrong of both our dads. I would never abandon my family."

"I know you wouldn't," she said, meeting his gaze. "That's not who you are. That's who they were. The three of you are different."

Dan looked in her eyes, his expression worn. He'd just dumped a heap of tragic family history on Gwen. Adding his speculations about Elena on top of it would be too much. As much as he'd tried to push Elena's startling confession from his mind, it kept sneaking back up on him, casting a weighty stone into the wellspring of happiness he was building with Gwen. This was the price Dan paid for letting a stunning woman get the best of him yet again. If nothing else, one good thing had come of his unfortunate Albuquerque encounter. He'd learned something about Elena once and for all. When that woman wept, she shed nothing but crocodile tears.

"I'm not sure if having kids is in the cards for me anyway," Dan said after a beat.

Gwen studied him with compassion. "I don't know much about cystic fibrosis, but I'm familiar with other hereditary diseases. It can't be a hundred percent chance?"

"There are very few full guarantees. There's prenatal testing you can do, but to what end? Would you want to have that choice put to you, Gwen? Whether or not to end the life of your unborn child because it might be imperfect?"

Gwen's head and heart swirled with confusion, the whirlpool of emotions threatening to drag her under. What a heart-wrenching scenario that would be for any potential new parents to face. "I honestly don't know what I think. I've been lucky, I guess. I've never had to deal with anything like that."

Dan's lips drew into a thin line. "Given the choice, I'd venture most women would prefer not to have to." He appeared distant, as if recalling an unpleasant memory.

"Well, maybe most women aren't smart enough to think things through. It seems to me that when a couple is in love and longing to build a family, there are many ways to work things out. Anyway, I believe that all children are special gifts, don't you? Just look at Jocelyn and the joy she brought to your life."

Dan studied her for a prolonged beat. There appeared to be a million thoughts racing inside him, but Gwen couldn't decipher a one.

"For a Carolina girl, you're an awfully wise woman," he finally said.

Gwen flushed at the compliment, understanding that things had deepened between them. Dan had opened up to her in unexpected ways and she was honored he'd felt he could trust her.

"Thanks for telling me about Jocelyn. Seeing as how our time together is so short, you really didn't have to."

"Precisely why going for quality over quantity is my aim. Since we've agreed to take this next little bit to get to know each other, I thought maybe we should begin by dispensing of secrets." He glanced at her wedding band, and Gwen felt her face burn hot.

After Dan's sincere confession, she felt like a big plucky chicken refusing to give him fair play in return. But Dan had worried over events that were really out of his hands. What did it say about Gwen that she hadn't even found the guts to deal with something on her own finger? Would he think her emotionally inept in accepting a marriage that failed, or worse yet, extra loopy for feeling she had to find just the right spot to shuck its golden albatross?

"I want to tell you, I do," she said hoarsely. "And I will, very soon."

It was a long, slow descent toward Santa Fe, the mountains opening up into the deep, craggy canyons of the Rio Grande River. Dan had taken this way home on purpose. He knew the perfect spot where he hoped to take Gwen and finally kiss her. Kissing that woman was long overdue, and Dan intended to make good on his earlier promise. He'd been incredibly impressed with how poised Gwen had remained in taking the news about Jocelyn. She'd listened intently and had absorbed his difficult story, offering insight and compassion. Elena and her hysteria be damned. There was clearly a woman who could love him better. Dan's throat swelled at the thought of the "L" word. The truth was he thought he'd sealed his heart off so it would never head in that direction again. But the more time he spent with Gwen, the more that restless stallion beat against the gate. And man, when Gwen smiled at him, didn't it itch to bolt into open pasture and run free.

Gwen surprised Dan with a shout, causing him to slam on the brakes. "Wait! Stop here!" she cried. "Pull over, please!"

Dan veered onto a wide shoulder on the road and downshifted, putting the car in park.

"Gwen, all you all right?" he asked.

"Can we park here a moment?" she asked with a hopeful blush.

Park? She wanted to park? This wasn't precisely the place he had in mind, but it clearly was no less beautiful. Dan surveyed their surroundings, noting theirs was the only vehicle within sight. "I'm sure that's fine."

Gwen stepped from the SUV onto a craggy ledge overlooking the Rio Grande. It was a spectacular sight, swelling as it flowed downhill from the southern edge of the Rocky Mountains. Up river, kayakers conquered white rapids, their paddles gleaming in the sunlight. "This is perfect. Absolutely perfect," she told him, her face beaming. She twisted the ring on her finger, more sure than ever. Now was the time, this was the place—in this beautiful New Mexico wilderness with this wonderful man. She looked up into Dan's questioning eyes colored like the azure sky above them.

"You know why I haven't taken this off?" she asked, holding up her hand. "Because I was scared, afraid of what I'd be without it. You see, all my life I've defined myself by someone else. I was Elizabeth's daughter, Marian's sister, Robert's wife... And Robert wasn't much of a husband."

Worry lines creased Dan's brow. "He wasn't...? He didn't hurt you, Gwen?"

"Physically, no. But if words were bullets, I'd be six feet under, that's for sure."

"I'm sorry."

"Yeah, well, I am too. Sorry and tired. But mostly I'm tired of feeling sorry for myself. Bad things happen to good people, right? We talked about that in Taos. I understand now that I'm not particularly special. I was just there, in the wrong place at the wrong time."

"And now?" he asked, kind eyes imploring.

"Now I'm right where I want to be. I like who I am. I'm not silly or stupid. My work isn't ridiculous. And you know what?"

Dan arched both eyebrows. "What?"

Gwen squared her shoulders and stood up a little straighter. "I think I'm interesting!"

Dan let loose a belly laugh, charmed and delighted by her. "I should say so! The fact of the matter is I believe you're the most interesting person I've met."

Gwen beamed from ear to ear, feeling as if she'd gotten hold of a giant balloon that was lifting her into space. "I'm glad that you think that, Dan. I find you pretty fascinating too." With that, Gwen centered the fingers of her right hand on the gold wedding band and gave it a tug. It rose to her knuckle and stopped. She tilted her head at Dan. "Want to help me with this? I think it's stuck."

Dan shot her a grin that sent wild butterflies fluttering. "That, Ms. Marsh, would be my pleasure."

Nesting her fingers in his, Dan helped her with a small jerk that sent the ring sliding.

Gwen shook her head sadly at the outdated piece of jewelry in her palm, then closed it in her grip. "You don't know how long I've wanted to do this," she said with a grin. And then, with a fierce, long lob, she sent it arching into the Rio Grande River.

"Hey, people!" Gwen shouted merrily at the kayakers, who probably couldn't hear her anyway. "I'm free! I'm totally free!"

They smiled and waved back at what they may have presumed to be a nutty woman, but Gwen didn't care. Suddenly, she felt Dan's arms around her as he pulled her close, snuggling her back against his chest. "I'm glad that you're free," he whispered, his breath tickling her ear. "I'd hate to think of myself as falling for a married woman."

He spun her to face him then, and Gwen knew she was in heaven, caught between the river and his stunning blue eyes. "I've waited a long time to do this," he said, his voice husky with desire.

Gwen was glad he'd steadied his arms around her, supporting the small of her back, because in this very instant she felt her knees giving way. Dan drew her closer, their mouths just a whisper apart. "God, you're a beautiful woman," he said, bringing his lips to hers.

At first, his kiss touched on her lightly, but then it deepened into a sweeping intensity that sent electricity rocketing through her. Her face was on fire, and her belly stirred with a primitive hunger that had nothing to do with food. Gwen wasn't sure how long they stood there on that ledge overlooking the Rio Grande. All she knew was that she thought she heard hoots and hollers and resounding bouts of applause echoing from down below them in the canyon.

## Chapter Eight

Dan's BlackBerry rang as they approached town.

"Good timing," Gwen said with a grin.

"Couldn't be better," Dan agreed, thinking that Gwen had picked an even better make-out spot than he'd planned. He must have enjoyed kissing that sumptuous mouth for over an hour. He just hoped those kayakers weren't uploading the event on YouTube.

"Hello?" he said into his phone. "Really? That's super."

"Megan says your canvases are in," he told Gwen. "Looks like everything arrived in order."

Gwen beamed at him as he quickly finished up, telling Megan they'd be by shortly.

"Mind if we stop by the gallery?" he asked Gwen, thinking she wouldn't. "I'd like the artist to double-check things personally. If it all looks fine, I'll ask Megan to come in early and hang them on the back wall as a series."

"Do you think Megan will care?"

"About getting up early? Yes, probably. About the extra bit of cash that will be added to her paycheck, not one bit."

Gwen laughed lightly in a musical way that Dan knew he could get used to.

"Thanks for taking me to Taos," she said, warm brown eyes sparkling.

Dan smiled softly at this sweet, wonderful woman. "I'm glad you had a good time."

A crimson blush streaked her cheeks. "I had better than a good time," she said seductively.

"Yeah," he said, already a bit wistful the memory. "Me too."

"Dan," she said after a bit, "is there something special I should wear?"

"Wear?" he asked, suddenly thrown off kilter by the change in tack.

"Tomorrow, silly. For when the buyers come by."

They came to a stoplight, and Dan scanned Gwen from her head to her ultra-sexy toes.

"It's a Friday, so we'll get more than our usual flow. It would be good if we could introduce you as our feature artist and have some sort of small reception."

"That would be lovely," she said with an excited grin. "Are you sure you can pull something together so last-minute?"

"Megan's very good at these things. She usually puts out wine and cheeses on Fridays anyway. No reason she can't add a fresh bouquet of flowers and scatter around some of your business cards. You do have business cards?" he asked with concern.

"Why, yes, of course! I made them on my home computer, so they're not the most professional, but they'll probably do in a pinch."

"That's excellent, then. Why don't you let me set the whole thing up and encourage any browsers who come by during the day to stop back in the evening to meet you?"

"Sort of like building suspense?" she said happily. "I like it! But you still haven't told me what I should wear?"

"Anything you're comfortable with. You might want to dress up a little but include something that shows your personal style."

"Like my new cowgirl boots?" she asked, arching an eyebrow.

Good Lord was she a sexy woman. One habañero-pepper-hot-looking woman. And she kissed like a house on fire. "Those would be fine," he said, cranking the AC up a notch.

Gwen was excited at the idea of a reception and still glowing from their kissing session by the Rio Grande. It had been a wonderful day, maybe even one of the best in her life.

"How many people do you think might drop by?" she asked.

"Somewhere between twenty and two hundred," he said with a grin. "I'm really betting my money on the women from Texas."

"Texas?"

"Two sisters out here on vacation and interested in making artistic investments."

Gwen thought of the toned, tanned, and lovely set she'd spied him talking to through the window. "Tall blondes?" she asked.

Dan's face scrunched up in a puzzled expression. "Yes, but how did you…?"

"Oh, I saw a pair like that perusing the galleries the other day. They did seem be carrying terribly big purses."

"Let's hope they hold awfully big wallets." Little lines tugged at the edges of his mouth. "In any case," he added, "I'm hopeful that tomorrow night will be a success. You'll accomplish your goal before going home." Gwen felt an immediate one-two punch to her stomach.

No sooner had he said this than he appeared to think better of it, pursing his lips.

"I'm sorry," Dan said quietly. "I didn't mean to…"

"It's all right," Gwen said, though her shaky voice betrayed her.

"Gwen," he said, reaching out and taking her hand. He held it firmly in his but couldn't seem to force out further words.

She gave his hand a tight squeeze, gathering her courage. Then, with shoulders back and chin raised, she said, "We both knew the timeline when we started."

Gwen never really imagined how horrible it would feel coming to the end of it. The girl who'd rationalized all that philosophical nonsense about stepping stones seemed a million miles away right now.

"I want to thank you again for everything," she said softly. "Selling those canvases for me is a big deal, probably bigger than you imagine."

"Then we're going to do it," he said firmly. He shot her a sincere look. "I won't let you leave New Mexico without what you came for. There may not be a lot I can promise you. But I can promise you that."

Dan sat gloomily at his desk, thumbing through paperwork. His and Gwen's incredible day trip to Taos had ended on an unexpected down note. But then, what had he anticipated? Did Dan really imagine that he and Gwen could remain in that blissful bubble of denial forever? First thing Monday morning, she was flying back to North Carolina. That had never been any sort of secret. Still, he'd let himself get caught up in the notion that it was only now that mattered. He'd gone so far as to entrust Gwen with his secrets and tell her about his family. She'd been amazing in how she'd handled things and then later had opened up to him. The joy that shone from her face when she'd tossed that ring into the Rio Grande River was nothing short of spectacular. Then there'd been that kiss to beat all kisses, the one that sent lightning raging through his veins and made him hungry for even more of her. But there was to be no more of her. Within another few days, she'd be gone. The sooner Dan set himself straight about that, the better.

Dan laid aside his papers as Megan bustled around the gallery, getting things ready. She'd done the hanging first thing, and everything looked superb, with Gwen's canvases showcased in an optimal spot beneath the skylights. Dan had already put in several calls but was only a third of the way through his list. Despite what he'd said to Gwen, he couldn't count on the Texas twosome to bite. From what he'd seen of them, they'd probably be more apt to, given competition. And if nobody came through, Dan had a backup plan. It was the least he could do. Besides, he'd already made a promise to Gwen.

"Megan?" he called out to her. "Can I speak with you a moment?"

She looked up from a huge vase in which she tastefully arranged flowers. "What's up?"

Okay, so he was determined to do it, but he didn't want to shout it across the gallery. "Could you, please..." He motioned for her to come over. "It will only take a second."

She stopped what she was doing and came and sat in the chair in front of him. "Is this something about the reception tonight? Because if you want me to stay late, the fact is I already came in early and—"

"No, not at all," he said, subverting her worry. "I'll stay and clean up. I wouldn't expect you do that on top of all you've already done." He gave her an easy smile, and she relaxed in her chair.

"Great! Thanks."

Dan laced his fingers together in a businesslike fashion. "The truth is I wanted to speak to you about the sale of Ms. Marsh's canvases."

"Yeah. They're pretty good, huh? I think they'll move, don't you?"

"I'm actually interested in guaranteeing that."

Megan scrunched up her pixie-like face. "Like how?"

Dan cleared his throat, trying to sound natural. "If all five haven't sold by nine fifteen—"

"All five? Do you seriously think that's possible?"

Dan sent her an enigmatic grin. "I'd say it's certain that all five will sell by nine thirty."

"Uh-oh, I smell subterfuge." She mulled this over a moment, then asked impishly, "What do you want me to do?"

Gwen sat in the cool quiet of her suite, sipping a rosehips-and-cinnamon tea. She'd walked around town for a bit to release her pent-up energy, but being out in the heat had only made her more anxious. She didn't know what she was nervous about, for heaven's sake. She'd had her work on display before and had spoken to people about it. Those other times were small events, though, and this was the big-time. This time, Gwen needed to walk away with a substantial cash sum. Gwen felt herself growing sweaty and instinctively reached to twist the band on her finger. She looked down with happy surprise, noting it was gone. Gone, chucked clear into the rapids of the Rio Grande River, never to be seen again. It had been such an exhilarating moment, yet in some ways she was numbed by it. Part of her still felt as if she were in a daze, unable to grasp that terrible phase of her existence was over.

Something she recalled with utter vibrancy was the way Dan had held her. Her senses tingled at the memory of the kiss that went on and on and on… Her first assessment of Dan as a world-class kisser had been right on the money. Gwen felt a tender ache in her chest. She was falling hard for Dan, but within another couple of days, she'd be gone. Just as they were really getting to know each, the fates would tear them apart, sending her back to North Carolina and Dan to his life on Paradise Ranch.

Gwen chided herself for the self-pity. She hadn't flown out here to fall in love. She'd come to sell her art, and hopefully this evening, that was exactly what she'd do. Gwen stared down at the empty spot on her ring finger, thinking of the hurt Robert had caused her. Now, completely without meaning to, someone quite the opposite, a true prince of a man, stood to crush her as well. Maybe getting involved with Dan had been the wrong thing. But the more she was with him, the more she wanted to be around him. This was sure to make it extra painful when she had to go. Gwen recognized the fullness in her eyes as welling tears. She set down her mug and dabbed them with a napkin, knowing she'd not made things any easier on herself.

It had been a wonderful week, but already she felt as if her heart was breaking. If she got in even deeper, Gwen didn't know how she'd extract herself. It had taken her nearly three years to get over Robert, and toward the end, she hadn't even cared for him! What sort of shape would she be in after finally finding the right man but at the wrong place and time? Gwen sucked in a breath, knowing she had to be strong. She had goals to achieve for herself and was on a serious mission to help her sister. If the canvas sales went well, perhaps there'd be more trips to Santa Fe and other opportunities to see…

Gwen folded her face in her hands as sobs escaped her. Who was she fooling with this? Did she really believe that would be good for her? Having an occasional long-distance romance with a man who was sure to forget her once she was out of sight and probably out of mind? She knew he meant well now. Dan was gorgeous and generous and kind. He was certain to have other women after him. As much as

Gwen believed he really liked her, she had to face facts. She was a big girl and old enough to understand she probably wasn't unique.

Gwen dried her eyes and lifted a magazine from the coffee table before her. *Santa Fean* magazine sat atop the large stack of local brochures and flyers left as a compliment in her guest room. She flipped through its pages, trying to distract herself from her crumbling emotions. Suddenly, he was right there in front of her. It was a picture of Dan by his horse on Paradise Ranch. "Best Billionaire Bachelor Catch in the West?" Gwen said. Rich? Dan was rich? She sat for a moment and absorbed this, the bitter truth sinking in. Instead of making things better, that somehow made them worse. The fact that Dan was wealthy only made him more generally appealing. She scanned through the quotes from local women talking about what a great guy Dan Holbrook was, and how every single gal within a hundred-mile radius was eager to date him. The women interviewed were doctors…lawyers…successful businesswomen. Gwen swallowed hard, knowing she couldn't compete. She was a stone-broke music teacher who couldn't even sing.

She read through the story about Dan's charity work with disabled children, her heart brimming with sorrow. He was an even more wonderful person than she'd imagined. There he was, someone who'd suffered privately in his past, and he'd turned the situation around so he could give back to others in spite of it. Gwen felt privileged to have known Dan in a more intimate way than any of the interviewed ladies had, but was equally devastated by what she saw as clear fact. She wasn't meant for Dan's future. With all the women in the state to choose from, why would he accept the complications of falling for someone living two thousand miles away? No wonder Elena had regretted their relationship ending. She obviously wanted Dan back and had tracked him down to tell him so. How many others out there were waiting in the wings, hoping to do the same?

Red flags went skittering up the pole, telling Gwen to guard her heart and step back. As memorable as her times with Dan had been, there could be no more like them. They'd made some picture-perfect memories in Santa Fe and shared an unforgettable, romantic getaway to Taos. That mental photo album would be Gwen's only keepsake of her relationship with the "Best Billionaire Catch in the West." She needed to prepare herself for that reality.

When Gwen arrived at the gallery, it had been transformed into a magical fairy realm, the parameters of its rooms strung with tiny, decorative lights. A side table held wineglasses and bottles, some of them chilling in buckets of ice. Platters of various cheeses and fruits were arranged strategically throughout, inviting guests to pause before particular works of art and graze while browsing. A selection of classical music played discreetly in the background, and fresh flowers were everywhere. Gwen made her way through the milling crowd, past clinking glasses, low chatter and laughter. A huddle of shoppers stood in the back gallery admiring Gwen's work and exchanging pleasantries about the powerful presentation, perspective, and use of color. Dan was nowhere in sight.

Gwen spied Megan with a small group near the pottery and went to thank her for the beautiful arrangements. Megan saw her coming and gracefully opened the small semicircle of patrons to include Gwen. "How great to see you!" she said, smiling first at her and then the others. "This is the super new talent I've been telling you folks about," she said to the others. "Ms. Gwendolyn Marsh."

Gwen willed away a blush, striving to appear professional. Yet when she spoke, she felt her voice tremble and her face grow hot. "Megan's very good at PR," she bantered cheerily.

The guests chuckled lightly; then each extended a hand, introducing themselves in turn. They had questions for her about her work, how long she'd been at it, and where she found her inspiration. It took her a while to answer them all, since each answer regarding inspiration was specific to a particular painting. Megan brought her a glass of wine and a small plate of food, and Gwen thanked her with a gracious smile, feeling her tensions ease. Speaking with these people wasn't nearly as intimidating as she'd thought. Everyone was so nice and appeared genuinely interested. Even those who might not have appreciated her particular style were far too polite to say so. The fact was this was a crowd that was interested in art, and that commonality bound them together, despite the fact that the bank balances of the browsers in here were sure to outnumber hers a hundred to one. The men were casually well dressed and the woman fixed nicely without looking overdone. Gwen glanced down at her flirty earth-toned dress and boots, hoping she'd chosen right. A whisper in her ear confirmed it.

"You look dynamite," Dan said, stepping up behind her.

A current rippled down Gwen's spine as heat centered in her belly. He was incredibly handsome in a sports coat overlaying a deep-blue polo. She turned toward him with surprise and suddenly felt light-headed. Was it him or those first two glasses of wine back at the inn? She scolded herself for pregaming, when the occasion was important as this one. At least she'd taken care to triple-check her hair for Havarti. "Dan! I didn't see you when I came in."

Dan had certainly seen her. He'd spied her the moment he'd stepped around the corner. She'd been captivating the group with her soft smile and subtle Southern accent. Dan noted a few of the men eyeing Gwen a tad too appreciatively and flashed hot at his nape. He was silly to feel jealous. She was a beautiful woman. It would be impossible for other men not to notice. Dan silently cursed himself for insisting she wear those sexy-as-all-get-out boots, then realized he was being absurd. He didn't have any sort of claim on Gwen. For some reason, that admission made him unhappy.

"I was just in the back gallery," he said. "There are a couple of folks in there dying to meet you, if you can pull yourself away?" He raised his brow at Megan, who picked up right away on his lead.

"Right. Ms. Marsh, why don't you run on ahead? I'm sure these good people will excuse you." Gwen said her good-byes to them, and they thanked for her time, saying what a pleasure it had been to speak with her. Dan noted she was exceptionally bubbly tonight, charming them all with her natural effervescence.

"They were nice," she said to Dan, her cheeks flushed with color. She really did look amazing. No wonder none of the guys in here could take their eyes off her.

"People always love talking to real, live artists," he said with a grin.

"As opposed to real, dead ones?" she asked pertly, pretty blonde curls playing about her face.

Dan repressed a smile, thinking she was being awfully plucky for someone who'd never worked a room like this one before.

Big brown eyes flashed up at him with innocence. "What? I understand that many artists are famous posthumously."

"Let's hope you don't fit into that category any time soon."

"Famous?"

"Posthumous."

Dan escorted her toward the back gallery, wishing she'd stop looking so damn cute and flirty. He found it almost aggravating of her to exercise her winsome wit besides. He was already growing agitated at the thought of her leaving. The overabundance of appreciative male gazes only made things worse. That signaled Gwen would have no trouble easily getting another guy. Dan paused, allowing Gwen to pass into the large anterior room ahead of him. She sashayed through the threshold with a sway to her hips and clomping cowgirl boots. Dan withdrew a hanky and dabbed the back of his neck, thinking someone had turned up the heat in here. That someone being Ms. Gwendolyn Marsh!

Gwen entered the anterior gallery and paused, clasping her hands to her chest. Her oils were skillfully hung on the walls and in a perfect arrangement. They looked so good it was almost hard to imagine they were hers and she was the featured artist!

Two tanned blondes turned from their study of her work, pivoting toward her on spiky heels. She recognized them at once as the pair from Canyon Road and the women she'd seen flirting with Dan through the window. Both held empty wineglasses and looked of the ilk that could hold their liquor.

"You must be the artist," the taller one said, exuding haute sophistication. "We've just been admiring your work." She extended her hand. "Victoria Kent. So pleased to meet you."

"You too." Gwen reached toward her, toppling slightly. Dan shot her a curious gaze as she drew in a breath and pulled herself up straighter.

"And this is my sister, Emily," Victoria said, introducing a shorter version of herself who ran about ten pounds heavier.

"Good to finally meet the infamous Gwendolyn Marsh," the other said. "Dan hasn't stopped talking about you." She looked Gwen up and down, then suggestively scanned Dan. "You must have made quite an impression on him."

Gwen felt her temples and cheekbones warm, sensing she'd been accused of something. She returned the woman's gaze with combative caution. She hadn't cared for Emily's approach but understood circumstances dictated civility. "I'd like to think Dan understands art."

"That I do," he said, graciously stepping in. "In fact, the moment I saw Gwen's oils, I said to myself, these works won't last long on the market." He smiled pleasantly at Gwen. "I'm happy to say my assessment was correct. We have a very interested buyer coming by at nine thirty."

Victoria flushed, perplexed. "But I thought you told me that these were available?"

"They are," Dan answered evenly. "No one has made a final offer yet."

"I see." Victoria exchanged glances with her sister. "If you'll excuse us for a few minutes. We'd like to talk something over."

"Of course," Dan said as the women retreated around the corner.

Emily lingered behind her sister, sending Dan a slow, sultry perusal as she went. Gwen felt her skin burn hot.

This was just the sort of thing that was destined to happen, over and over again, the moment she left town. "I think that Emily's more interested in the gallery owner than my art."

Dan released a surprised laugh. "What? Are you kidding me?"

"Come on Dan, you can't pretend you didn't see her give you that once-over?"

"You're besmirching the good name of a happily married woman." Little lines tugged at the edges of his mouth as blue eyes crinkled. "Besides, I'm not even the gallery owner. But only you know that," he closed with a wink.

He was an impossibly maddening man. More maddening than Gwen had given him credit for. Either he was totally obtuse to attractive women hitting on him, or he was trying to deflect the situation by making light of it. "I don't think it's your artistic assets she's interested in."

"Whoa! Hold the phone. You couldn't possibly be...?"

She crossed her arms in front of herself, that beautiful mouth drawing up into a pout.

"What?" she asked, with defiant dark eyes.

He couldn't believe it, but it was true. "Jealous," he said in a whisper. "Oh...my...God!" Dan slapped his forehead for emphasis, then lowered his voice. "I can't believe it. You're actually jealous of her...?"

"No, Dan," she spouted in hushed tones. "I'm not jealous. I just don't appreciate her flouncing in here like this were some sort of club instead of a real business establishment. She nearly devoured you with her eyes, for heaven's sake! 'Mrs. I Come from Texas but Want a Big Night with a Big Man in the Big Town'!"

"Santa Fe's not that big."

"Oh, stop it," she said, losing patience. A sheen overtook her eyes, and Dan suddenly feared he'd pushed her too far with his teasing. "All you can do is make fun…"

Gwen turned away and set her chin to keep her jaw from trembling. She was on the verge of breaking down into a cascading waterfall of tears. How exactly professional was that? What was she thinking anyway? Of course Emily had ogled Dan. What woman in her right mind wouldn't? Although Gwen would certainly thank them to keep their overt appraisals slightly more discreet. Emily had looked Dan over like a juicy tenderloin steak fresh from the fire. She'd even licked her lips, for heaven's sake. Like she could practically taste him! Gwen squared her small shoulders, devising her plan. If the woman didn't have enough to eat, Gwen would help her. "I'll be right back," she told Dan, striding past him and into the next room.

Dan followed Gwen into the open space, concerned by the look on her face. He'd seen those gorgeous dark eyes spark with fire once before. The last time, the ammo had been aimed at him. Dan watched Gwen make a beeline for a small snack table stacked with plates and fruits and cheeses. Perhaps she'd grown hungry or faint, Dan thought hopefully. Gwen's gaze homed in on the Texas twosome standing nearby with replenished wines, and Dan changed his mind. He didn't know what Gwen was up to, but the way she clip-clopped purposely across the room told him no good.

He frantically scanned the gallery for Megan and gratefully caught her eye. Dan held up his BlackBerry and motioned moving forward with the other hand, telling Megan to speed up the time line. She raised her finger in understanding and quickly set to the task. But even

Megan's keen mental abilities and efficiency weren't enough. Dan hustled to the small table where Gwen was heaping mounds of food upon a flimsy plate. "I insist," she said to Emily with a broad grin that appeared slightly manic.

"Not so much cheese," the Texan protested. "I'm watching my waistline."

Gwen arched both eyebrows and momentarily stopped heaping. "Oh, are you really? That's too bad." She smiled sweetly at the statuesque Victoria, who'd already fixed herself a healthy plate. "Let's take some tips from your sister, then. Shall we? The Southwestern Ranch dressing on celery sticks is to die for!"

Dan grimaced at Megan, who hustled over as Gwen dropped spoonful after spoonful of creamy, white dressing onto the overloaded plate.

"That's really quite enough," Emily protested as Megan cut in.

"Mr. Holbrook,!" Megan said, holding up the house phone.

The group angled toward Megan, startled by the distraction.

"Oh dear!" Gwen cried, tipping the unsteady plate in Emily's direction. Emily looked down in horror as streams of Ranch dressing raced down her dress.

"It's designer!" she shrieked, grabbing for napkins.

Dan handed her some more to help. "So sorry!"

"I feel so stupid," Gwen said. "I don't know how that happened!"

"The gallery will pay for dry cleaning," Dan offered to Emily.

"Thanks," she said, still mopping herself up. "Let me hit the restroom and see what I can do."

Dan directed his gaze at Megan, wanting to somehow salvage this evening. It was the first time he'd ever seen the young girl look flustered. He hoped she'd still be able to pull this off. Things surely weren't looking good in the selling-to-Texas department.

"Mr. Holbrook," she uttered weakly, still holding up the phone. "The gentleman who was in earlier today wants to put in a bid on the Marsh series."

"All five?" Gwen asked, elated.

"That's quite a lot," Victoria added.

"He's willing to pay top dollar," Megan said. "Four thousand a piece."

"Four thousand!" Victoria exclaimed. "But each is only marked at three-five."

"Plus gallery commission," Megan added, as if reciting from memory.

"What's that?" Victoria inquired of Dan.

"Twenty percent. Another four thousand dollars." Dan smiled pleasantly all around. "If you'll excuse me," he said to the group. "I think I'd better take this call."

"Wait!" Victoria said, blinking hard. "I'd like a chance to make an offer as well."

"Would you?" Dan asked, stunned as Emily returned still a royal mess.

"What's going on?" Emily asked.

"Somebody's trying to outbid me," Victoria said, as if it had never happened before.

"No! We've already been online and scoped out new swags and fabrics for the rooms."

"Yes. Ones that will complement this theme exactly," Victoria added.

"Gwen?" Dan asked, turning to her.

"Well, it seems to me if we have such a spectacular offer… Four thousand a piece, plus the gallery commission…"

"I'll match that!" Victoria cut in. "In cash!"

"Cash?" Dan asked with surprise.

"The banks open for a few hours in the morning. I can get a cashier's check or make a wire transfer."

Gwen's lovely face lit up like a thousand fireworks on the Fourth of July. She turned eagerly toward Dan and nodded with a heartwarming grin.

"We'll take it," Dan said, shaking Victoria's hand.

Megan handed Gwen a cup of coffee with a smile. "Creamer and sugar, two packs."

Gwen flushed with embarrassment, thinking of the display she'd put on. She hadn't precisely been drunk, but she'd clearly been tipsy. What else would excuse her utter assault on Emily's wardrobe, designer or not? "I feel like I should be helping you," she told Dan as he carted empty wine bottles to the recycle.

"No worries at all," he told her with a sincere twist to his lips. "Nancy's trained me right. I'm used to this."

"It's true," Megan assured her. "Dan's a real sweetie about picking up. He always tries to make Friday evenings so he can help out."

"I thought you didn't usually do much with the gallery," Gwen said, surprised.

"Popping by once in a while and schmoozing with the art scene isn't much of a hardship." Dan exited to the back room, and Megan smiled after him fondly.

"He's really pretty cool for an old guy."

Gwen couldn't help but grin at Megan's youthful assessment. Dan didn't seem old to Gwen at all. He was aged just right. He was a great guy too. Just look at all he'd done to help her and how smoothly he'd help negotiate that deal. It hadn't been under the most stellar circumstances, Gwen thought, a wave of shame overtaking her. She was ashamed of herself for acting out so badly, and all because some woman had made eyes at someone who wasn't even her man!

"Coffee all right?" Megan asked with big, wide eyes.

"Yes! Just fine," Gwen said, taking a sip.

Dan came back in, and Megan gathered her things. "Still okay if I knock off now?" she asked him.

"Of course," he told her. "You've more than earned your bonus."

"Bonus?"

"Don't think you won't be rewarded for all the help you were today."

"Why, thanks," she said with a wide, happy grin.

Megan whistled merrily and pranced out the door with all the vim and vigor of someone who'd never known the hard burdens of life.

Gwen set down her coffee as Dan lowered the blinds. "Are you sure there's not something I can do?"

"You can tell me how excited you are to have sold all your canvases," he called back with a smile.

"I am excited," she answered honestly. "No, excited's not strong enough. Try over the moon."

"Ecstatic, huh?" he said, pivoting toward her.

"Yes, that too." Gwen took a deep breath, gathering her nerve. She'd made such a spectacle of herself, she couldn't just sit here and act like it hadn't happened.

"Dan, I need to apologize for my...clumsiness tonight."

"It was an accident, surely."

"Absolutely! Never even saw it coming," she said, quickly biting her lip.

Dan studied her a prolonged beat.

"I guess what's important is that everything worked out."

"It did indeed! Wait until I tell my sister."

"Marian? I'm sure she'll be very proud of you."

Gwen faltered a moment, unsure of how much she should say. Now that the deal was nearly closed, she reasoned it wouldn't hurt anything to let Dan in on her motivation behind this venture. He'd been such a champion and so totally upfront with her about so many things, where was the harm?

"Marian's actually the reason I came here," she said.

"Beg pardon?"

"She's in very bad straits, Dan. Financially, I mean. Totally at risk of losing her house."

"That's terrible." His eyes flashed with alarm. "Does she have a family?"

"Five kids and one on the way. No husband. The ex is actually sort of who helped cause this mess."

Dan's expression grew cloudy. "Why am I not surprised?"

"In any case, she needed a certain amount of money to get out from under the thumb of her creditors and to make do until she's able to start working full-time."

"Twenty thousand dollars," Dan said, more a statement than a question.

"Exactly."

He took her in again, his gaze filled with admiration. "You're a very special person, you know that?"

She warmed under the heat of his stare, but her heart, reawakened by the sudden burst of caffeine, said beware.

"I think you're special too, Dan. I could have never imagined coming here and meeting such a wonderful person. You've made my stay in Santa Fe very memorable."

"I'll never forget these past few days either," he said. Gwen could tell by the look on his face he wanted to step forward and close the distance between them. Yet she viewed a telling restraint in his eyes. He'd been thinking just what she had. This unforgettable interlude between them was nearly done.

The bell tinkled above the entrance, and Dan turned toward the door in surprise. Elena stood there in casual elegance, a designer scarf draped strategically around the sleek line of her neck. "Don't tell me I'm interrupting," she said, her words a sledgehammer to Gwen's chest.

"I'm afraid you are," Dan said, his tone not the least bit friendly.

"Well, then, I guess that's just too bad." Elena strode forward and thumped a thick white envelope against Dan's chest. "Family first. Isn't that your motto, Dan?"

Dan pushed the envelope aside, eyes narrowing. "What's going on here, Elena?"

"You wanted proof," she said. "I brought it. The blood work's all in."

Dan knitted his brow and contorted his lips in shock. "I don't believe you."

"Then read this," Elena said, slapping the envelope sharply to his desk.

Gwen's heart swirled with emotion as her face burned hot. "You're not...sick?" she asked.

Elena turned toward her, indignant, then spouted back, "As a dog. That's what morning sickness does to a woman."

Gwen felt her knees wobble and sat unsteadily in a chair as Dan ran a hand through his hair. Dan's words came back to her like loud, clanking cymbals. *I would never abandon my family…"* "It's true?" she asked him, unable to mask her disbelief.

Dan met her gaze with shameful apology. "Gwen, I'm so sorry. I didn't know until…"

"Why are you apologizing to her? Don't you and I have a few things to talk about?" Elena demanded harshly.

Gwen could see through the windows it was still a vibrant evening, passersby in huddles mulling down the street. She fought the fire in her throat as heat welled in her eyes. "I'll see myself back to the inn," she told them, rising. "It's only two blocks away."

Dan studied her with a remorseful longing. "I'll call you in the morning with the purchase confirmation."

"Don't bother," she said, heading for the door before her heart could completely burst open. "You can just send a text."

Dan read through the medical report in stunned silence. "I thought you said you were on the pill?"

"Was on the pill, Dan. I mean, while we were dating. After we stopped, I stopped."

He met Elena's catlike green gaze. "So last month in Albuquerque…?"

"That's right."

Dan ran a hand through his hair. "But I wore protection."

"I guess it wasn't foolproof."

Dan sat heavily in his chair, his heart sinking. This couldn't be happening. Not now, not with Elena.

"I want you to know that I'm keeping it," she said flatly, as if expecting no reaction.

Dan pursed his lips, then looked her in the eye. "That's the right thing to do."

"I didn't think I'd want… I mean, back when were together, I said…"

Dan noted the fine creases rimming her eyes. "You said a lot of things, Elena."

"I know, and I apologize for a lot of them."

"Only a lot?" he asked, raising his brow.

She seemed suddenly exhausted. Fragile. She stared up at him, green eyes imploring. "For everything, Dan." Her bottom lip trembled as she fought back tears. "I'm truly, truly sorry for everything. Don't you think there's maybe a way…? This has got to be some sort of sign. You told me yourself, no baby's an accident."

Dan felt helplessly confused, his world falling apart. For the past few days, all he'd considered was how to go about building something special with Gwen. Now that dream seemed as elusive as some forgotten illusion from his tainted youth. Dan stared at Elena, his heart searing. He was not his father, would never in a million years be anything like that man. And when his mettle was put to the fire, Dan was going to have to prove it.

# Chapter Nine

Gwen got a text from Dan saying he'd stop by the inn around noon to drop off the check. While she understood it was the quickest way to get the money, she knew it would be difficult seeing him in person. She'd spent a horrible, sleepless night reliving Elena's unwelcome entry. It was more like an intrusion, really. A disruption that had totally upended Gwen's world and any ridiculous dreams she'd had of forming a lasting relationship with Dan. Gwen shook off the morning chill and took another sip of coffee from her steaming mug as she sat by the inn's kiva fireplace. In the winter, she knew it was a blazing hearth and this town an enchanting wonderland. She'd seen the photos of luminaries strung from trees, their cheery glow resonating from every rooftop. She'd secretly hoped to have a reason to return, perhaps ring in the new year with Dan. Now that fantasy appeared absurdly unlikely.

Gwen scolded herself for her down mood, reminding herself to be grateful. She hadn't come to Santa Fe to fall in love. She'd come here on a mission to help her sister, and that goal had been miraculously satisfied. Expecting that her own personal fulfillment would somehow profit from the situation was beyond sophomoric. This afternoon, she'd scout the town for small souvenirs for Elizabeth, Marian, and the kids. Then tomorrow she'd take in one last museum and finish packing. She'd have to make it an early night, since her Monday-morning flight left at seven and she had the rental car to return beforehand. Gwen smiled sadly at the empty spot on her left hand, understanding her time in the New Mexican sun was nearly done.

She took in her surroundings, knowing she was going to miss it here. This had been a valuable trip, in more ways than monetarily. After years of uncertainty regarding her bad breakup with Robert, she'd finally gleaned the clarity to understand herself. Gwen now believed that she was a worthy and likeable person. She'd also developed a newfound strength. While she might be leaving Santa Fe with a heavy heart, she was also departing with a firm resolve. No man would ever take advantage of her or make her feel inferior again. She now knew who she was, and she loved that person. Others might love her or not, but that would never again change her own perception of herself. Gwen squared her small shoulders and sat up a little straighter in her chair, finally believing herself capable of facing anything, even saying so long to Dan.

Gwen sat in the inn's lobby on one of the big, comfy sofas, a sun-bleached deer skull over the kiva fireplace before her. Dan walked in and saw her sitting there as beautiful as daybreak. Sunlight streamed in through low-hung windows, catching the gold in her hair. Gwen heard his approach and turned big, dark eyes upon him. Eyes that made him wish he could turn back the clock and undo so many things..

He came and sat beside her, tapping his suit pocket. "Our Texas Twosome came through," he said, fighting the shake in his smile. He extracted the bank envelope and passed it over.

"I can hardly believe it," she said, bringing a hand to her chest. Chocolate-brown eyes brimmed with gratitude. "This will make such a difference to so many people," she said.

"I know," he answered kindly. "But mostly I'm glad to see it make a difference to you."

She opened the envelope and withdrew the cashier's check, a trickle of moisture escaping her eye. Dan reached up and gently stroked her tears back with his thumb. "Eyes as beautiful as yours don't deserve to be crying," he said, still cupping her cheek.

"But these are tears of joy," she said, collecting herself and dabbing her eye with a tissue.

She met his gaze with a seriousness that almost broke his heart. "How's Elena? Did the two of you work things out?"

Dan swallowed hard past the burn in his throat. "We're discussing what might be best for the child."

"Of course."

Dan held her gaze. "I promise you, Gwen, I didn't know. Had no clue about the baby when I met you."

"I could tell the news came as a shock."

Dan cleared his throat. "Yes, well. Some things in life just do."

"Yes," she said sadly.

Dan rose slowly and held out his hand. "It's been a pleasure, Ms. Marsh."

Gwen stood and took his grip. "The pleasure was all mine," she said, her voice trembling.

In spite of himself, he pulled her to him, the sweetness of her form molding to his one last time. Dan shut his eyes against the ravages of heartbreak, holding her tighter than ever.

"Good-bye, cowgirl," he whispered into soft gold curls. "I'll never forget you."

Gwen spent the rest of the afternoon touring the town and picking up presents for her family in North Carolina. It was good she'd mapped out the day in advance. Otherwise, she wasn't sure she could have gotten through it. Already, she'd memorized this city's map, and her familiarization with its landscape helped her navigate the canyon stretching wide in her soul. Gwen ached from the inside out at the chasm that had been newly inserted between her head and her heart. While she understood and respected Dan's choice, she couldn't help but mourn the loss of the fabulous fantasy that a man as incredible as him might somehow be hers.

Gwen rounded the bend to Loretto Chapel, a deep melancholy taking hold. Oh, stop it, she told herself, bucking up. There were plenty of gals out there who'd never even tasted the wonder of Dan Holbrook's kiss. She'd been lucky enough to have him hold her, actually care something about her. His feelings had been authentic, of that much she was sure. She couldn't blame him now for doing the honorable thing. That just further proved he was every bit the responsible party she'd always believed him to be. Gwen squared her small shoulders and stood a bit straighter as she entered the chapel gift shop. She'd purchase a small refrigerator magnet of the "Mysterious Staircase" as a reminder of the memories engendered here. She'd never forget Dan either.

Dan massaged his jaw as he studied the doctor's report Elena'd left with him. While everything seemed in order, why did he have the gnawing sensation that something didn't add up?

"Guess I'll be taking off for my six weeks' vacation now," Megan said with a bright grin and a flip of her pixie bangs.

"What's that?" Dan asked, looking up. Megan was poised to go, that enormous bag strung from her shoulder.

"You can't tell me you've forgotten?" she asked with a blink. "Justin and I are going camping in the mountains, then heading up into Calgary for a while. You said it was all right, that you'd double-checked with Nancy—"

"Yes, yes," Dan reassured her, rushing in. "Of course, I remember now. I'm sorry, Megan. I've just had other things on my mind."

"Oh Gawd," she said with a sparrow-like gaze. "Please say it's not Elena."

"Say that what's not Elena?" Dan asked, perplexed.

Megan crossed petite arms over her boyish chest. "This thing that's gotten you all wacky," she replied. "Like you don't even know what day of the week it is, for instance, and can't recall you've given me six weeks off."

Alarm bells rang in Dan's head. Six weeks! Oh…my…God. Dan rescanned the data on the doctor's report, verifying. Elena was eight weeks along. The baby couldn't possibly be his.

He sprang from his chair, startling the sparrow by wrapping his arms around her. "I love you, Megan!" Dan said, giving her a firm peck on the cheek.

She squirmed a bit in his embrace, then worked free, massaging her upper arms. "Geez, Dan. I think you're cool too. But not like that, okay? I play with kids my own age."

"Of course you do," he said, feeling as if he was sporting an idiotic grin. He laughed out loud then, releasing the joy and relief of it all. "Of course you do, Megan. No doubt!"

She blinked twice, thickly painted lashes nearly sticking, as Dan withdrew his billfold and pulled out a wad of cash.

"What on earth are you doing?" she asked, taken aback.

Dan's grin stretched so wide, good God, it nearly hurt. "Thanking you, little darling. Thanking you sincerely." He shoved the cash in her hand, then waved her outside. "Go on, now. You and Justin run off and have a marvelous time."

She stared at him like he'd gone positively mad, then rushed out the door, her huge bag flying behind her. "Thanks, Dan! Thanks a lot," she said, not daring to look back.

Dan brought two hands to his head, running his fingers through his hair, a whole new world of possibilities opening up. He broke out laughing again, perhaps like a lunatic hyena. But he didn't care. No sirree, he definitely didn't care. That smart little gallery assistant had just granted him a new lease on life.

"I'm flattered you'd drive all the way to Albuquerque for coffee," Elena said, her cheeks taking on a rosy hue. Maybe she was glowing or whatever in the world it was that pregnant women did.

"Elena," Dan said, unfolding the doctor's report on the café table between them. "There's something I've got to ask you about this."

Elena sat back in her chair, clearly shaken, as if he'd accused her of something. "I'm not lying about this, Dan," she said, her voice atremble. "The results are authentic. You can speak to the doctor yourself if you'd like."

"That won't be necessary."

"Then what…?"

"I noticed something on the printout I think we should discuss."

She tilted her chin and gave him a wary gaze. "Okay…" she said, drawing out the word.

"This date, Elena. Right here. What does it mean?"

She glanced at the paper, then met his eyes. "Approximate gestation?"

"Eight weeks!" he proclaimed firmly. "It says eight weeks! Don't you see what that means?"

She looked down at the document again, then slowly raised green eyes to his. She took a short breath, the shock of the truth hitting her. "Oh no. No, no, no... That can't be."

"There had to have been someone else. You told me so yourself you were off the pill."

"No, no, no..." she repeated, as if she hadn't heard him. "Not my junior assistant!"

"Who?" Dan asked, surprised.

Elena gritted her teeth, then grimaced. "He's very young and very hot and, kind of like, works for me."

Dan swallowed hard, playing his best poker face. "I'm sure it's not the first time it's happened."

"But we didn't do it after you and I... I mean, I told him that I couldn't. You were the last, Dan. I swear."

"But apparently not the most important," he noted astutely.

Elena folded her face in her hands and moaned.

"Is he any good?" Dan asked.

Elena stared at him between splayed fingers. "That's an inappropriate question!"

Dan flushed. "I meant as your assistant."

"Oh, that..." Elena released a tense breath. "Yes, yes. He's very good. Excellent, actually. Ivy League quality."

"Good genes, then," Dan said, fighting the grin tugging apart his lips.

Elena straightened herself tersely, folded the doctor's report three times, then tucked it in her purse. "I hope you're not disappointed," she said, eyebrows arched.

"Uh...maybe just a little," Dan fudged, feeling as if his spirit were flying.

"I'm sorry, Dan. I truly never thought. The guy always wears protection… I mean, there were only a couple of times. Just a few times in Denver…and that once at the office." Elena gasped and brought a hand to her mouth, realizing she was prattling on.

"Appears you have a lot in common," Dan said, picking up his coffee cup. "You probably won't mind if I take mine to go?"

She'd gone positively beet red, a color he didn't know she was capable of. "To go sounds fine, Dan. Just fine. Fine and dandy. Best wishes to you."

"To you too, Elena," he said, standing. "You and the…family."

He bowed and took his leave, scurrying out of there lest his luck might change. Good God Almighty was that poor young buck in for a surprise. Dan exited onto the street, greeting the first passerby he met with a grin. "I'm not the daddy!" he proudly proclaimed. "I'm not the daddy!" he hooted again into the air. Panic dawned as Dan checked his BlackBerry. Gwen was due to leave for the airport within the hour.

## Chapter Ten

Dan screeched into the circular drive as Gwen exited the inn, her luggage in tow. She stared in disbelief as he stepped from his SUV and raced toward her. "Gwen," he cried, his tone tinged with desperation. "You can't go!"

Gwen set down her bags and looked at him with incredulity. She wore tight stretch jeans, a sexy-as-all-get-out peasant blouse and those hot-as-Hades turquoise-trimmed cowgirl boots. "What do you mean?" she asked, dark eyes flashing.

"I'm not going to be a daddy! Not now, not with Elena." He heaved a deep breath. "Not ever with Elena, thank God."

Gwen stared up at him, beautiful chocolate-brown eyes softening. "You're not?"

Dan slowly shook his head, fighting every inner instinct he had to pull her into his arms and kiss her soundly like she definitely deserved.

She searched his face with a kindness he found utterly irresistible. "Something terrible hasn't happened?" she asked with concern.

"Something wonderful's happened," Dan said, quickly correcting her. "Elena and I... She and me, we..." He exhaled deeply, letting the whole truth out. "It was somebody else, Gwen. Another man is the father. The timing doesn't add up. Please don't misunderstand me, I'm far from perfect. Very far, actually. Pretty imperfect if you think about it—"

She brought a delicately sculpted hand to his chin to stop him. "You're not upset about this?" she said in her soft, Southern twang. "I mean, disappointed about not becoming a daddy?"

"No," he said firmly.

"Well, then," she asserted brightly. "This is probably good news."

"Better than good," he assured her, "the very best."

Gwen set a hand on her hip and gazed up at him, setting forth a challenge with her dark eyes. "And what, pray tell, do you plan to do with it?"

"Invite you to Paradise Ranch?" he said with a squeak.

Gwen glanced down at her suitcases. "It would have been good to have the invitation a day ago, or even two."

"Be fair," he said, beseeching. "Up until this morning, I thought I was…in a family way."

She shifted on her feet, considering his proposition. Her jaw was set, but Dan could tell her resolve was crumbling. He gave her his best charming grin. "You can't leave Santa Fe without seeing its most stellar attraction."

"Does this mean there will be starlight involved?"

"It might."

"But my plane reservation," she said, indicating her bags.

"I'll book you another."

"You or Holbrook and Holstein?" she asked with a saucy tilt of her chin.

He stared into hypnotic brown eyes, wanting so badly to up and carry her away.

"Me, Gwen. Dan Holbrook. The invitation is not professional. It's strictly personal."

A beautiful smile broke across her sensuous lips. "Well, then," she replied, handing him a bag. "It would be impolite of me to refuse it."

Dan cranked the ignition and wheeled them out of the city, the adobe-toned town fading behind them. Rolling hills dotted with sage brush and pine peaked higher as narrow buttes towered toward the sky. They passed one spectacular mesa after the next, their magnificence lording over the twilight as the sun sank low behind the Sangre de Cristo Mountains.

"How far outside of the city are you?" she asked.

"About eighteen miles. We'll be there any minute."

Gwen was over the moon, a billion thoughts and feelings racing through her head and heart. Paradise Ranch! Dan's private sanctuary. He was actually taking her there. And much better than that, oh, so much better, was the fact that he was totally free. Gwen didn't know the details about what had transpired with Elena, and in many respects she didn't want to. The idea of Dan being with another woman in the most intimate way was not a thought she wanted to entertain. Gwen wanted Dan to be hers and hers alone; she sensed that in her soul now more than ever. She thrilled at the thought that he might feel the same about her. Wasn't his taking her to Paradise Ranch proof positive of things moving forward?

Gwen wasn't sure how to phrase it, but she was dying to know more about the camp and the children who might be there. It was awkward, though, because Dan hadn't yet said anything about it. Surely, it wasn't some sort of secret. Dan's philanthropic bent had been profiled in the media, for heaven's sake. Should she tell him she'd read *Santa Fean* magazine and that she knew all about him being the "Best Billionaire Catch in the West"?

"Will anyone else be joining us?" she finally asked.

He wrinkled his brow, appearing genuinely confused. "I'm sorry?"

"Out at the ranch. You know, the others… Little people?"

Dan released a belly laugh. "Are these like midgets or Lilliputians?"

"Dan! I'm asking about the kids!" she said in frustration.

He turned to look at her a prolonged moment, then centered his eyes on the road. His lips pulled into a hard line as he appeared to think this through. "So you know about the camp."

"I didn't think the information was classified," she answered honestly. "It's in prominent magazines, for heaven's sake." Gwen felt her cheeks flush. There, the truth was out.

Gwen cast her gaze on Dan, seeing he'd reddened from his open collar up. Even the tips of his ears were crimson. "You read the article?" he asked, giving her an embarrassed glance.

"In the *Santa Fean*, yes."

He firmly gripped the wheel. "Oh God."

"I was very impressed," she told him. "Seriously, Dan. I believe it's a wonderful thing you do for those children. I don't understand why you wouldn't want me to know?"

"I did want you to know. In fact, I'd planned to tell you tonight."

"Will I be meeting any of the campers?" she asked hopefully.

"I'm afraid not, Gwen. The camp runs in two sessions. Two weeks after school gets out in June, and then the first two weeks of August. With the timing of your trip, you've just missed it."

Gwen felt the corners of her mouth take a downturn. She was genuinely disappointed. "That's too bad. I'd really hoped… I mean, I thought it would be fun… What I'm trying to say is that I love being around children. I'd actually gotten myself geared up and was looking forward to it."

Dan studied her with pleased surprise. "Were you really?"

"Why, yes. Yes, I was."

"You're very special Gwen. I'm sorry you missed this round of campers. I know the kids would have loved you too. Maybe we can see about it some other time?"

Some other time? Was Dan indicating a future, or merely being polite? "Yeah," she said uncertainly. "That would be great." Then the deeper part of the reality set in. No camp plus no campers meant that they would be alone. "So, nobody else will be there, then? Out there on Paradise Ranch?"

"Gwen, if you're starting to change your mind..." he said kindly. "I honestly don't mind driving you back." He checked his BlackBerry. "If we rush, you can probably still make your plane."

"No! It's not that..." she started badly, then was totally unsure about how to finish. What could she say? *I don't trust myself around you and that hot body, when you're bound to also have a hot bed?* Her fantasies about becoming intimate with Dan had been so wonderful up until now, mostly because that was just what they were. Was Gwen really ready to face that reality? Her plump little...uh...large rear matched with his hard-toned thighs, nothing but skin between them?

Dan knitted his brow, looking gloomy. "It's the money thing, isn't it?"

"Money thing?"

"You read what those other women said about me. You probably think I'm some kind of playboy and don't have intentions that are sincere."

Actually, Gwen was more worried about herself than him. While his good looks and wealth might make him appear to be the playboy sort to the general public, Gwen had gotten to know Dan privately. She trusted her instincts when they said he was nothing of the sort. He wasn't the type to take advantage of people. Everything she'd learned about Dan had shown him to be caring and kind. When she first met him, he'd also had a completely guarded heart. His heart seemed to be opening up just as much as hers. She could tell by the hurt in his voice and the pain in his gaze. He couldn't stand for Gwen to think poorly of him, for whatever kind of reasons he might imagine.

"I don't think that about you at all," she assured him. "I may not know you as well as I'd like to, but I've definitely seen enough to have a sense of who you are."

Relief washed across the lines of his handsome face. "Then, you haven't changed your mind?"

Butterflies alighted in her stomach as her heart galloped into overdrive. "I'm yours for the night," she said, smiling softly. The tips of Dan's ears flushed crimson again, and she quickly turned away, directing her gaze at the stunning New Mexico landscape. "Or the rest of the afternoon," she continued hastily. "Or until whenever you decide to book my new reservation."

When she turned back toward him, he shot her a smile and a brief glance. "I should think you'll have some say in the date of your return reservation as well."

"Why, yes. Sure. Of course." Gwen mentally kicked herself and vowed to quit babbling. Maybe if she sat extra still to enjoy the view, Dan would magically forget how moronic she'd sounded.

Dan kept his view on the road, not daring another glance at the sensuous woman beside him. Had she intimated what he'd thought? Was Gwen hinting that she'd sleep with him? It wasn't like it hadn't crossed his mind. From the moment he'd tasted Gwen's ultra-hot lips, he'd known that kissing wouldn't be enough. He longed to hold her and take her completely, losing himself to her feminine warmth. Dan couldn't wait to get home and slip into a pair of jeans and a comfortable shirt. He tried not to envision Gwen taking them off slowly, disrobing him as he watched.

"Look out!" Gwen shrieked.

Tires squealed as Dan swerved to avoid a jackrabbit. "Sorry about that." He grimaced, steering them back on the road. Gwen had her hands pressed to her heart like she thought he was about to drive them off a mountain. Maybe he was. Perhaps this whole thing was crazy. Him and Gwen alone on Paradise Ranch, his big bachelor bed just sitting there—empty, cold, and lonely. He'd be damned if he didn't want to, but could he really do that to her? Gwen was so wholesome and trusting. He doubted she'd been with a man since her divorce. It wouldn't be right of Dan to take advantage of that, with the future between them still so uncertain.

A lump welled in Dan's throat as he thought the whole thing through. He couldn't stand the thought of Gwen leaving and not coming back. Even if she came back, he wasn't sure how he'd endure her absence in the interim. All Dan knew was that he needed to be with her, now and possibly long after that. The sun sank over the mountains, streaking the sky with a grenadine hue. It was a beautiful summer evening and would be a crystal-clear night. There would be over a billion stars around. Dan was going to make good on his promise to Gwen that she'd see them.

Dan turned off the main road and onto a gravel drive. He pulled up to a wooden gate and put the SUV in park.

"We're here?" she asked, fine color gracing her cheeks and temples. She was beautiful this evening, more lovely than he'd ever seen her.

"Welcome to Paradise Ranch," he said with a smile.

Dan rolled down his driver-side window and punched numbers into a keypad.

The enormous wooden frame of the gate swung open on giant hinges.

Gwen grinned as they passed under the stenciled wooden sign identifying Dan's private sanctuary. While he'd had occasional women since his big breakup with Elena, he'd never brought any of them here.

"I love it!" Gwen's face shone with delight as the winding gravel drive shaded by trees opened into the wide expanse of hills. High atop the highest one sat the rustic expanse of the main house. Other outbuildings dotted the surrounding area, including the camp dormitory, mess hall and barn, complete with a full-scale riding ring. At the edge of the pasture beyond, sat a low-roofed stable. "You can't possibly keep all this up by yourself? Even when camp is out."

"I've got some good hands around to help me," he said with a wink. "Trustworthy folks who look after the horses and such but don't sell my stories to the media."

"Are any here tonight?"

"Some will be around. But they heard we were coming. They'll keep their distance from the main house."

Gwen blushed wildly like the blossoming red yucca hedging the drive. She was one hell of a good-looking woman, and she was looking better all the time.

Grocery sacks rustled in back as they climbed the steep hill to their destination.

"So what's for dinner?" she asked sweetly.

"It's a surprise." Dan hoped that Gwen liked surprises and that she really liked spicy food as much as she claimed. He had a real treat in store, fresh from the land.

"I adore surprises," she said with a big, lovely smile. "The hotter, the better!"

"I'm not going to ask how you did that," he said, unnerved by her uncanny mental telepathy.

"I saw you eyeing those jalapeño plants," she said with a laugh.

He repressed a grin, charmed by her. Dan hadn't even realized he'd glanced at the side garden, mentally calculating how many peppers to bring in.

"You're one smart woman, *Ms.* Gwendolyn Marsh."

She squared her small shoulders and tilted up her lovely chin.

"Thanks! I appreciate you saying so."

Dan led her in through the great room, a rustic common area with an ample stone hearth, hardwood floors, and exposed beams in the vaulted ceiling. Three-hundred-and-sixty-degree views of the surrounding mountains were afforded through enormous windows. Gwen caught her breath at the panorama's beauty, as the grenadine sky faded to purple dusk.

Gwen shifted the purse on her shoulder. "It's incredible!"

"Thanks. I like it."

He carried her small overnight bag ahead of her, leading her past an open kitchen with a central island. Gwen was impressed to see a good arrangement of hanging pots and pans, and baskets brimming with fresh fruits and vegetables on the gleaming marble countertops.

"Who does your shopping?"

"I called ahead and made some arrangements."

She stopped walking and set a hand on her curvy hip. "So you were quite certain I'd come, were you?"

"I spent the better part of my drive back from Albuquerque hoping," he said with a grin.

Dan pushed back the door to a magnificent bedroom with views even more majestic than the ones from the great room. Gwen's purse slid from her shoulder and hit the floor with a thud. "Wow."

"The bathroom's through there," he said, indicating the far end of the room. "I've only got three bedrooms, but they're good-sized."

Three bedrooms were all you needed to start a family, Gwen thought, immediately startled that the idea had raced through her mind. She could imagine what an amazing place this would be to raise children. It was gorgeous, the air was clean, and there was plenty of running space all around. "I love Paradise Ranch, Dan. You've built quite a place."

"I'll show you the rest of it tomorrow. It's a little dark out now for the grand tour, but there will be time in the morning. That is, if you can give me the whole day."

Gwen ached to give him more than one whole day. How about the week, a month, a year?

Dan set her suitcase on a large blanket chest. "You're probably good and hungry. If you'd like to settle in, I'll go start dinner."

"Thanks! I'll be there in a second to help you."

"I'd like that," he said. "See you in a bit."

Dan shut the door behind him, leaving Gwen alone with her racing heart. What was she doing? Contemplating children in this house? Her children and Dan's…? She recalled how hesitant he'd been to tell her about Jocelyn's condition and the chance of it being genetically passed on.

If things were to progress and become serious with him, was this something that Gwen would be willing to face? She sat heavily on the bed and stared out the windows at the darkening sky. Of course she would, and in her heart, she knew it. Even initially put off, Elena had been willing to brave the odds once she'd believed her feet held to the fire. How could Gwen not step forward and be willing to take a chance, any sort of marvelous chance, to build a future with such an incredible man?

Gwen had never even considered having kids with Robert. It hadn't taken long for things to sour between them, so she hadn't exactly felt in the baby-making mood. But Dan wasn't Robert at all. Dan was wonderful and generous and kind. Gwen believed without a doubt that he'd make the most terrific father. She looked down at the empty spot on her ring finger, thinking she was blowing things out of proportion. It had taken her almost three years to shuck the bad marriage, for heaven's sake. What made her think she might be ready for another one?

She heard Dan whistling brightly down the hall as he banged about the kitchen, and couldn't help but smile. Here was a man who had everything. He could even carry a tune. Gwen stood from the bed and went to freshen up in the bathroom. She needed to wash her face and make a fresh start, forget all about futures and making babies in New Mexico. Thinking nonsense like that could totally spoil her enjoyment of the moment. She'd accepted Dan's invitation to Paradise Ranch in order to live for the here and now. Gwen had already wasted too much time living in the past. She wasn't about to let pie-in-the-sky ideas about Dan ruin her prospects for a pleasant evening.

She strode purposefully past the blanket chest, her purse with its emergency stow of makeup in tow. She couldn't help but wonder what it would be like to fill that cherry chest with a full layette in pale yellow, and nestle a bassinette in a sunny spot beside that broad window… Gwen raced for the sink and splashed cold water on her face, over and over again, until she felt the common sense flowing back into her. Gwen hadn't even believed she'd had a biological clock inside her! Now that she knew it was there, how could she get the blasted thing to stop ticking? Dan was thrilled beyond belief to be off the prospective-daddy hook with Elena. There were no indications in sight he'd be willing to become a father with her.

Gwen unzipped her makeup case, thinking she looked a mess. Here was the girl with Havarti hair who the incredibly gorgeous "Best Billionaire Catch in the West" had decided to ask over for dinner. She felt her cheeks warm, wondering what it was Dan saw in her. With so many women to choose from, he might have picked anyone. But he hadn't, she thought, enjoying the play of a smile on her lips. He'd chosen *her*. Gwen busily got to work repairing her face, lest she delay and Dan second-guess his decision. There was one thing Gwen was sure of. She wasn't going to let Dan regret taking her to Paradise.

Dan smiled at Gwen as she entered the kitchen. "I was just starting to miss you." She looked cuter than ever in jeans and those rocking boots.

Her ivory skin flushed deep rose. "Sorry if I took a bit."

"Not at all! You're timing's perfect. I was just about to toss the steaks on the grill. Let me pour you a glass of wine, and you can come join me."

"Sounds great." Beautiful dark eyes searched the kitchen. "Something smells delicious. What's cooking?"

"Homemade mashed potatoes with fresh-pressed garlic and chives from the garden, sliced summer tomatoes, and rib eye steaks on the grill with a skewer of hot jalapeños."

"Also fresh from the garden, I'd guess." She smiled, genuinely pleased. "Oh, Dan, my mouth watered just hearing the description."

He cocked his head at her and grinned. "I'm glad you approve. I'm happiest when my houseguests are happy."

"And I'm happy you're such a good host," she said as he filled a goblet with red wine and handed it over. She tasted it and licked her lips, lips so enticing Dan was itching to kiss them. Big brown eyes sparkled with delight. "Say, this isn't...?"

"Yes, ma'am," he told her with a grin. "The same wine we shared the night we discussed Loretto Chapel."

She lowered her eyes, then batted them over the rim of her glass. "As I recall, it's also the night we discussed miracles."

In spite of himself, his voice grew gravelly. "Yes, it was."

Dan sensed a rush of heat flow through him like lava. There she stood in those impossibly sexy boots...with that knock-your-socks-off body...and that come-and-get-me-and-kiss-me-all-over face. It took all the strength Dan had to resist sweeping Gwen off her feet and carting her down the hall to his comfy, king-size bed. God, he loved this woman, and he was going to tell her, show *and* tell her, good and soon.

"Want to join me on the patio?" he asked, picking up the tray of steaks to carry outside.

"Can I bring something?"

"Just your wine and that skewer of jalapeños." He cautioned her as she lifted the pepper plate. "Be sure not to touch any. You might regret it later."

She cocked an eyebrow. "More than the chile rellenos in the park?"

Dan released a belly laugh. "Very much more. These home-grown babies are a hundred times hotter."

"Excellent," she said with a big, appealing grin.

An hour later, they sat at the patio table, enjoying the view of the darkened valley and the aftermath of a superb meal. Gwen studied Dan relaxing with his wine. He was so handsome and at home in his element out here on the ranch. Gwen found it hard to believe what a lucky woman she'd been. She'd come to Santa Fe to sell her art and had somehow given away her heart in the bargain. It wasn't a bad trade. Gwen knew that if she had to do it over, she'd make all the same choices again. Getting to know Dan and spending time with him here in New Mexico had been one of the most memorable occasions of her life.

"Dinner was the best, Dan. Outstanding. Thank you so much for bringing me here. This has been a wonderful way to wrap up an unforgettable trip."

"It's not over yet," he said raising his glass to hers.

"No, it's not," she said softly. In many ways, Gwen wished it would never end. How incredible it would be if there was a way to freeze time and keep things just as they were—right now—forever.

The wind picked up, raking against them. Small chill bumps rose on Gwen's flesh, and she crossed her arms in front of herself to warm them.

"If it's too cool for you, we can go indoors," he said, noticing.

"No. I like it out here. It's beautiful," she said, studying the sky, which was studded with stars and a faraway moon.

"Then let me bring you a jacket," he offered. "Did you pack one?"

"I'm afraid not," she said. While it had cooled down at night in the city, it hadn't been quite as chilly as this.

"No worries," he said with a grin. "You can borrow one of mine." He added a sly twist to his lips. "Besides, you'll need it when we go riding."

"Riding?" Gwen asked with surprise.

Dan motioned toward the heavens above them. "You think the stars are spectacular now, just wait until you see what I've got in store."

He disappeared into the house and left Gwen's heart beating a billion miles per second. She didn't know where he was taking her, but she couldn't wait. If it involved this awesomely incredible man and gazing at stars, she was in.

Dan emerged in the threshold, dressed in a light leather jacket. He brought another one to her and helped slip it on. Its warmth engulfed her, and its clean masculine scent hinted of Dan. She zipped it in front of her, eager to go.

Little lines tugged at the edges of his mouth as blue eyes crinkled.

"Ever been on a horse?"

## Chapter Eleven

Dan led them down the narrow path to the barn, their way guided by starlight and the wide beam of Dan's flashlight. "Take my hand. It'll be safer."

Gwen settled her grip in his, her heart pounding. She always felt safe with this man. He was so capable. From ordering wine to running a place like this one, he always knew just what to do. She studied his profile in the soft light, thinking how carefree and youthful he appeared. He obviously loved being out on the ranch, but what about his regular job? How did he fit it all in?

"I don't know how you manage it," she said, a little breathless. Her short legs raced to keep up with his long strides. They were like young lovers stealing away in the night, hurrying off to their hide-away.

"I'm sorry, Gwen," he said with concern. "Do you want me to slow down?"

"No," she said, meaning it. How she wanted him to pick up the pace and keep on going, right to the point where he hoisted her up on a horse. Gwen's heart stilled, and a lead weight settled in her stomach. She'd never been on a horse before. She was such a klutz. What if she fell off? "About the horse, Dan…"

"What about him?"

"Is he a good boy? Nice and gentle?"

"Naw. He's a real spitfire. Full of vim and vigor, just like you."

She swallowed hard and stopped walking. He stopped as well and turned expectant eyes on hers. "How do we know I won't fall off?" she asked, her chin trembling slightly.

Dan laughed, giving her hand a tight squeeze. "Because I'm going to hang on to you," he said with a wink. "Don't worry, sweetheart. I'm not about to let anything happen to you."

Gwen's heart warmed at the endearment as she felt her face flash hot. She didn't know how she could find Dan more wonderful than he already was, but every second he seemed to be just getting better.

When they got to the barn door, he paused with a question. "What was it you were asking me? About how I manage something?"

She was so lost to the canyon of his gaze it took her a moment to remember. " Oh! I was asking about this… The ranch, the camp. All of it. I don't know how you find time for everything, running the gallery for Nancy on top of your day job too."

He gave her a warm, even smile and gently stroked her chin with his free hand.

"First of all, running the gallery's only temporary. Secondly, my day job's not nearly as demanding as it used to be. Holbrook Designs does custom jobs, each of them pretty pricy and lengthy to complete. I've got some really great people at the top that take care of most of the day-to-day for me."

"Do you ever get out on the sites?"

"All the time. There's nothing more exciting than watching one of ours go up." His gaze trailed back to the main house.

"Wait a minute," she said with delight. "That's one of yours?"

He nodded with pride. "I always do the final walk-through myself. Nothing I build gets declared done until I put my stamp of approval on it." His eyes poured over her, capturing her in their depths. "Although I haven't been out much lately. Between the gallery minding and other things, I've had different priorities in mind." He gave her a sexy grin that sent her pulse racing and made her feel overheated in the warm leather jacket.

A horse whinnied loudly, and she laughed with joy. "That must be your spitfire."

Dan pulled back the barn door and led Gwen to a stall housing a commanding chestnut Arabian stallion.

"He's beautiful," Gwen said in awe.

Dan warmly patted the horse's neck, then stroked down his mane. "How you doing, you old rascal, you?" The horse affectionately nuzzled him, and Dan laughed, the two of them pair bonded together.

"What's his name?"

"Rascal."

"Really?"

"It's the God's honest truth, isn't it, boy?" he said, patting the horse again. Rascal snuffled closer, inserting his nose in Dan's coat pocket. Dan raised his brow at Gwen, then withdrew the handful of carrots he'd placed there. "Always one step ahead of me!" Dan chuckled as Rascal gobbled up his treat.

"I'm starting to see where he got his name," Gwen said with a grin.

Dan shot Gwen a smile that set her tailbone tingling. He was phenomenally handsome standing there with his horse. She couldn't wait for them to carry her away.

"Okay, cowgirl," he said, "ready to ride?"

"Whoa, boy!" Dan steadied Rascal under the fine cast of starlight. They stood in the riding ring just outside the barn. "Just do what I told you," he instructed Gwen. "Grab on to the saddle horn there, put your right foot in the stirrup, and then hoist yourself up."

Gwen was a little worried about being all the way up there by herself. "Rascal's not going to take off running before you get a chance to join me?"

Dan chuckled and lightly patted the saddle. "No worries, little lady. You'll be fine." Gwen felt her face flush as she struggled with the stirrup that kept swinging away from her. "Here you go," Dan said, holding it steady for her.

Finally, she got her foot inserted, but it was an awfully big hop to the top.

"Need a boost?" he asked.

"Maybe a small one."

Gwen felt firm hands around her waist. "Now," he said. "Pull up." Gwen felt her other foot leave the ground as he lifted her with incredible ease.

Suddenly, she went soaring onto the saddle, her left leg swinging over the other side of the horse.

"Don't go anywhere," Dan said with a wink. "I'm coming right behind you."

In an instant, he was mounted at Gwen's back. He adjusted himself in the saddle, then scooted her toward him, securing her against his chest with his left arm. Gwen felt happy and wild and free out here in this desolate darkness with her rugged rancher man.

"Best settle in for a while, Ms. Marsh," he said, hugging her to him. "You're in for quite a ride." With that, he gave a loud command to his horse that sent the animal trotting.

Gwen's heart raced in rhythm to Rascal's hoof beats as they moved along the mountain trail that carried them northward. As they distanced themselves from the ranch's outbuildings, a huge sky opened up into an arching one hundred and eighty degrees. Billions of constellations appeared to compete with each other to take up dark space.

"I've never seen so many stars," Gwen said, breathless at their beauty.

"That one up above is Polaris, the North Star, and that one over there," he said, pointing toward the horizon, "is Venus, the Morning Star." He held her a little tighter, his voice a whiskey whisper in her ear. "Venus is the goddess of love, you know."

Gwen caught her breath and held it. Was he saying what she thought he was? "That's what I've heard," she answered, leaning back into him. Was it her imagination or could she actually feel his heart pounding beneath their thin jackets?

Dan rode them to an overlook that overhung the hills below them and positioned them perfectly beneath the open sky. "Want to hop off for a moment?" he asked.

Gwen nodded, unable to find her tongue. She'd never felt so much emotion for someone, or from them either, she thought, glancing in his eyes as he helped her dismount.

Once on the ground, Dan led her away from the horse and into his arms. "I'm so glad that you came here," he said. "Came away with me to Paradise Ranch."

"I wouldn't have missed this for the world," she said, gazing up at him.

He settled his palms on her cheeks, then brought his lips to hers and kissed her sweetly.

"Gwen," he said, his voice husky in the shadowy space between them. "My dear, sweet woman. How did I ever get lucky enough to meet someone like you?" He kissed her again, and this time his mouth lingered.

Dan trailed his fingers through her curls, lightly strumming her nape. He pulled back a bit and dove into her eyes with his, their souls melding in the warm heat between them. "I have to tell you something," he said. "Something important." Gwen's pulse rocketed. She didn't realize until now how desperate she was to believe… Nor had she truly understood how deeply she felt it.

Dan drew her body up against his with one strong arm and cradled her chin in his other hand. "I didn't mean for it to happen. In fact, I tried my damndest to avoid it. But the truth of the matter is it was useless. All my efforts came to one end." He gazed at her deeply, his eyes midnight blue in the starlight. "I've fallen in love with you, Gwen. No holds barred, one hundred percent, absolutely, positively in love. It's a feeling I thought I'd never find again, and one I've never felt so deeply."

Gwen tilted her chin up toward him, powerful yet helpless in his arms. She was not the weak, confused woman she'd been when she came here. She was strong now and sure of herself. What she knew most definitely was that she was head over heels, desperately in love with this man. That rendered her powerless to fight against those emotions. She could no longer deny what had been building in her heart all this time. "I love you too," she said softly. "More than I ever thought I could love anybody."

His mouth hovered over hers as he brought both arms around her, holding her close. "You don't know how happy I am to hear you say that," he said, closing the distance between them. He kissed her with a passion then that caused her to feel light-headed and hot all over. She wrapped her arms around him as he held her tighter, their whole hearts, souls, and hungers pouring into their kiss.

Rascal stomped on the ground and whinnied loudly.

Gwen pulled back and grinned. "He's not jealous?"

"Doubt that," Dan said with a chuckle. "He's got his own little filly friend back at the barn." He studied the horse, who was growing agitated. "Probably just cold, tired, and hungry. How about you?" he asked, jostling her playfully in his arms. "Ready to head back?"

"That depends," she said, cocking an eyebrow. "Will there be this kind of kissing back at the house?"

Dan grinned and playfully patted her rump. "That can be arranged."

Fire shot through her veins and heated her belly. It wasn't only kissing she wanted to do, and Dan's patting her backside had driven that message home. Gwen wanted to be with Dan as completely as a woman could be. He loved her, and she utterly adored him. She ached for them to be closer than mere kisses. As hot and wonderful as those were, she knew now they could never be enough.

Dan lightly stroked her cheek with the back of his hand. "Penny for your thoughts, cowgirl?"

"I was just thinking about how wonderful you are," she said with a grin. She stood up on her tiptoes and gave him a quick, firm kiss on his ultra-sexy mouth.

"Oh, good. That means we're on the same wavelength."

He gave her a quick peck back, then took her hand in his. "Rascal's getting restless," he said, leading her back to the horse. "Probably misses his filly," he said with a wink.

Their trip back to the barn was even better than their journey out here. There was a new closeness between them as Gwen settled into Dan's arms and they rode at a steady pace descending the mountain trail. She felt warm and safe nestled up against him, and the beauty of their surroundings was spectacular. The heavens twinkled above them like a black-satin sheath studded with diamonds. Cool breezes blew, rippling her hair and raking her senses with the scents of wildflowers and desert sage.

Gwen wanted to freeze this moment in time and stay out here with Dan forever. This wasn't just any ranch; it was like their own private paradise, a special place made for just the two of them. While Gwen knew it was loaded with campers during certain months, that didn't negate the sense of privacy this vastness leant, no doubt the whole year through. This space was a bounty of wilderness and natural beauty so rich and raw it almost hurt to absorb it. There was so much to take in, from the gorgeous mountain peaks to the surrounding flat-topped mesas and impressive cylindrical buttes. To see them in the moonlight was both eerie and breathtaking at once. Gwen felt as if she'd been transported to a fantasy realm, one utterly in contrast to the small East Coast beach towns she knew.

Gwen had never seen anything quite so romantic or been with a man she adored more. Dan's kisses were hot and wonderful, and he'd said he loved her. She felt heady from the moment and the swirl of emotions churning inside her. When Dan had pulled her to him, she'd wanted nothing more than to feel closer still. Gwen was glad she'd waited for the right man and the right time. She felt her heart unfolding like a flower emerging from a frost and into the sun.

"Still doing all right?" he asked, his breath tickling her neck.

"Perfect," she said, smiling back at him. "I love it here."

"I'm glad," he said, tightening his arms around her.

Dan dropped Gwen at the main house before riding Rascal back to the barn. He thought she'd be more comfortable waiting for him there, plus he needed time to sort through his thoughts. The way Gwen kissed him on the trail had set his heart on fire. She was so warm and yielding with that incredibly sensual mouth, her hot, curvy body molding against his. Dan had held her to him, his hands exploring the subtle lines of her nape, waist, and back.

He'd ached to investigate further and taste that delectable neck, trailing his kisses down even farther. Heat tore through him like a wildfire out of control. He gripped the saddle with tense thighs and steadied the reins in one hand, unzipping his jacket with the other.

Gwen loved him. She'd said it as much with her eyes as with her words. That knowledge gave wings to Dan's heart and caused it to soar. He couldn't recall ever feeling emotion this intense for a woman. Gwen was gorgeous and funny and smart. She had a hard-edged sass about her but could be sweet and sensitive too. She likely employed those skills as a schoolteacher, allowing her to be both firm and kind to her students. Dan thought of his Paradise campers, positive they would adore Gwen. She'd be good with them too.

Dan swallowed hard at what he'd been thinking. He wasn't just dreaming of sleeping with Gwen; he'd mentally started planning their future. Dan glanced back over his shoulder at the main house, its windows warmed cheerily from the lights indoors. He'd built that place as a bachelor pad but now was starting to envision it as something more. In his mind's eye, Dan saw children there, and not ones from the camp. There was a pretty, curly headed little girl rushing into his arms and calling him Daddy.

"Whoa there, buddy!" Dan said aloud, as much to himself as to his horse. Rascal obediently came to a halt, and Dan dismounted. Could he really be thinking about marriage and kids with Gwen? Dan had been forced to confront those thoughts with Elena, and they'd pained him deeply. Feeling as if he might be pinned to a woman he didn't love for the rest of his life had filled him with an overwhelming despair he feared he'd never escape. He'd hoped that over time, and in the common interest of the child, things between him and Elena might change, that he'd somehow grow to love her in an appropriate and respectful way. Then again, he worried he might not. It was to be an uphill climb with those unrelenting memories of one very kissable cowgirl hovering over him for eternity.

Dan glanced back at the main house, wondering if the idea of having a family with him had crossed Gwen's mind. He understood how hard it was for her to trust somebody again. She'd been through a horrible marriage, and it had taken her all this time to recover. She'd let down her guard and allowed him into her heart, nonetheless. It was written in those beautiful brown eyes every time she looked at him. Nothing in the world could disguise it, and nothing in the universe made Dan happier.

Yes, he wanted her, damn it. He wanted her not just with his heart and soul, but with his body too. He swore that if he got that woman under the covers with him, it would be about a week before they ever came up. Dan would have to call in a cook and housekeeper as reinforcements. He'd be mighty obliged to arrange it too. But was being with Gwen now in that way the right thing? She'd endured so much hurt for such a long while. Dan didn't know whether she'd kissed a man since her ex. He had an even stronger suspicion she hadn't slept with one. This made it all the more important that if Dan and Gwen were to get together in that way, Dan had to make damn sure the moment and circumstances were right.

# Chapter Twelve

Gwen nervously checked her hair in an oval mirror surrounded in New Mexican tile. It hung in the passageway leading from the great room to the kitchen and stood beside the coatrack over which she'd draped her leather jacket. Her cheeks were still flushed pink from the night air, and her hair had been tousled by the wind. Gwen's skin warmed at the memory of Dan's touch. His fingers had raked through her curls, then traced the line of her back as his hungry mouth overtook hers. She recalled barely having the strength to stand in his arms. If there'd been a place for him to take her and lay her on the ground, she would have let him. Gwen strode to the kitchen and fixed herself a glass of water, her face and chest flashing hot.

She hadn't felt these yearnings for a man in such a while, she couldn't name the last time. It had to have been with Robert, and back at the beginning. That beginning was so hazy now, she felt as if she were examining it through a clouded glass. Even if she'd wanted Robert then, those impulses had nothing on the raging pull she was experiencing now. With Robert, she'd in many ways been a girl, a college kid engaged to her first love. Tonight, she was a woman with the accumulated experiences that had made her both jaded and wise.

She also was no longer attracted to a boy. She'd found a mature man, someone who was strong and caring. Dan knew himself and was sure of who he was. Gwen found his self-assurance and masculinity unbearably appealing. Plus, he had those unbelievably gorgeous eyes and that incredibly sexy twist to his lips that he revealed each time he was teasing. Dan lightened Gwen's heart and made her laugh with joy. She'd never felt so much happiness around a man, nor had been made to feel at greater ease.

Gwen anxiously paced the kitchen, hoping Dan would offer her at least one glass of wine. As much as she wanted him, she couldn't help the tiny knot that was forming in her stomach. While she was certain that Dan would be gentle and loving, she still experienced some minor nerves about them finally being together. Would he love her body just as much out of clothes as in them? Although she suspected he longed to be with her just as much, would he feel the same about her once it was done? Robert hadn't done much to inspire her confidence in that department. Just as he'd accused her of failing at everything else, he'd said she hadn't done much for him in bed either.

Gwen glanced down at her empty ring finger, upset with herself for letting Robert intrude on her life even now. It was high time she fully trusted that Dan and Robert were different. Dan would never say the hurtful things to her that Robert had. He loved her with his whole heart. Dan had said it, and Gwen believed it. From the top of her head to the tips of her toes, Gwen longed to give herself to Dan. She ached to take from him too. She wished to explore every inch of his toned and masculine body, first with her hands and then with her lips. She'd bring her mouth to his and kiss him deeply as he centered his hands on her hips. A brushfire ignited at Gwen's breasts as she felt the heat spread lower. She had to sleep with Dan or go crazy. She'd never wanted anything more in her life than she wanted him tonight.

Dan entered as Gwen was cleaning up the kitchen.

"You don't have to do that," he protested, hanging his coat on the rack.

"I don't mind, really," she said with a smile. "Besides, it's almost done."

Dan looked around the gleaming kitchen, appreciation settled into the rugged lines of his face. "Thanks, Gwen. That was really nice of you."

"It was no problem," she said. "You took care of Rascal; I took care of this."

He strolled to the center island and pulled two bottles from its built-in rack. "Can I offer you a glass of something? Wine? Whiskey?"

"Whiskey!" she cried with surprise. "I'd better not." She'd seen the effect the tequila in that avocado margarita had on her. Gwen decided she'd be safer sticking with a lower-alcohol-content drink. "I'll take some wine, though. Are you offering red or white?"

"Your wish is my command." Dan gave her a sexy grin that sent her heart cartwheeling.

Gwen pursed her lips to stop herself from saying something foolish. She could think of lots of things she'd like to ask him to do, none of which were proper. "Which are you drinking?" she asked.

"Either's great with me, as long as I can sit down and kick off my boots. Bet you're ready to get out of yours too."

Gwen's heart raced into a gallop as he uncorked the wine. Already he was thinking of undressing her. "My feet are a little sore," she offered, hearing her own voice squeak.

He raised his brow. "Need some water?"

"Got it," she said, awkwardly lifting her filled glass from the counter and nearly dousing her shirt. She inhaled a quick breath and set it back down without taking a sip.

Dan eyed her curiously as he poured their wine. Gwen accepted her glass, her hand trembling. Maybe she'd been out in the night air too long. The altitude had gone to her head, then shot straight through to other regions.

"Are you all right?" he asked sincerely. "You look like maybe you should sit down."

And she felt like it, too. The closer he got to her, the more she thought she would pass out. Faint from the nearness of his hot, masculine self. Gwen didn't know how she'd make it through but was determined to stay strong. He was so god-awful beautiful there had to be a law against him, maybe even in several states.

"Come on," he said gently, taking her elbow. "Let's just ease you down on the sofa, nice and slow." He held her wine until she settled in, then handed it back to her. "Maybe the horse riding was too much for you. I shouldn't have kept you out so long."

"No! I wanted to stay!" She felt her face flush hot, embarrassed that she'd sounded like a crushed-out teenager. She took a long, steady swallow of wine, then looked up, trapped in his gaze. "That makes two of us," he said. "Unfortunately, Rascal didn't agree."

Dan went to get his own wine, then came and sat beside her, taking her hand.

"Gwen, sweetheart," he said gently. "You can relax. It's just the two of us here."

That's precisely what she was afraid of. Him… Her…. And, eventually, no clothes between them. Gwen wasn't sure if she was ready for this.

"Let me help you with those boots," he said, bending forward and gripping the left one. Gwen squeezed her eyes shut and lifted her leg, letting him take it off. She sighed with relief, realizing how much the boot had been pinching. "Better?" he asked.

Gwen nodded numbly. This was the beginning of the end, and she knew it. First came the boots, then the shirt…next the jeans… Of course, he'd be taking his off too. Gwen felt woozy, the room suddenly whirling around her.

Dan tugged off her other boot, studying her with concern. "I think maybe we'd better nix the wine," he said, lifting the glass from her hand.

"It's okay," she said, grabbing it back. "I like it,"

Dan pushed back against the sofa and crossed his arms over his broad chest. "Sweetheart, you mind telling me what's going on?"

Him calling her sweetheart was one of the nicest things she'd heard. Gwen knew she could get used to it. She could get used to a lot of things with this man. Some of them might take more practice than others. It wasn't her fault that she was rusty. "Nothing. Nothing at all. I'm just recovering from the ride."

"Good," he said, bringing his arms around her and pulling her close. "For a moment there, I was worried you'd grown tired of kissing."

"I'd never grow tired of that," she said weakly as his mouth closed in.

He kissed her gently at first and then passionately, pressing his firm chest up against her. Her world spun out of control as her wants fought with her reason. She needed him so desperately, simply had to have him. Yet something deep inside her was just as desperately afraid. If she took this next step and became intimate with Dan, how would she handle it if he somehow went away? Would she someday look back and wish they'd never been together at all? Would that prove one more memory that would simply cause heartache?

Dan paused to stroke her cheek. His gaze was all smoke and fire, sultry and hot like a Santa Fe afternoon. "Honey," he said, his tone growing gravelly. "You don't know how much I love you, how much I want to be with you."

Gwen swallowed hard, steeling her courage. "I want to be with you too."

"I know you do, cowgirl. Believe me, I can't wait." He smiled at her and gently kissed her lips. "But I think that we ought to."

"What?" she asked with surprise.

Dan took her hand in his. "Listen Gwen, I know this is all moving pretty fast for you. We've just admitted how we feel about each other. There are things we need to work out, like when we'll see each other again and how we plan to manage our relationship."

Gwen's heart leapt with joy. This wasn't only about her trip to Santa Fe. Dan was talking about a *future*. He was so wonderfully understanding and kind, Gwen could scarcely believe she'd been blessed enough to find him. Overcome by emotion, love, and longing, she felt the tears spring from her eyes. "I'd like that very much," she said, her chin trembling. "I don't want this to be over."

Dan steadied her chin in his hand and moved in for another kiss. "Sweetheart," he said, drawing closer. "We've only just started."

He kissed her then, over and over, with a tender passion that assured Gwen everything would be all right. Here was a man who loved her and would watch over her heart. She didn't know where the next step would lead, but as long as it was a road that she and Dan could travel together, she was willing to take it.

Hours passed, and their kissing turned to holding, then the holding turned to dozing…at least on Gwen's part. Dan stared down at her angelic face, cheeks dusted light pink as she slept cradled against his chest. It felt so good to hold her. It was like she belonged here, like she'd always belonged here, with him, in his arms.

He'd seen the relief wash over her when he'd told her they wouldn't sleep together. He repressed a chuckle at the irony that she was now sleeping on him. "My dear, sweet woman," he whispered to her. "I've waited a lifetime for you. Did you think I couldn't wait one more night?" She stirred slightly, and he held her more tightly, sensing in his heart he'd never want to let her go.

The truth was waiting one more night had been difficult for him. It was painful in more than just a physical way. Every one of his manly urges had insisted they be together. Reason had said waiting until Gwen was completely sure would make things that much more wonderful for both of them. Dan would never do anything to hurt Gwen or cause her regret. He needed her to trust him with her heart and soul. Once she did that, he had faith she'd trust him with that beautiful body too. Until then, he had to act like the mature individual he'd always told himself he was. For the moment, he was just happy to have her close.

His heart thumped in his chest at the recognition that he might have never met her. Serendipity was a funny thing, and a happy coincidence had placed Gwen in his path. Had Nancy not gone to France on her honeymoon, Dan wouldn't have been overseeing the gallery. Hell, if Nancy hadn't gotten engaged, she would have never left town. Love was unusually cryptic in how it brought people together. It was like a huge jigsaw puzzle filled with blotches of color that didn't make sense until the individual pieces fit together and you saw the big picture.

Dan looked down at the incredible woman resting in his arms, knowing this was the portrait he wanted. He tried to paint it in his mind's eye lest he forget. Dan shook off the feeling of panic that swelled his throat. Forgetting Gwen would mean that she'd be out of his life, and he absolutely couldn't have that.

"Dan...?" she called drowsily, raising her head. "What time is it?" Gorgeous dark eyes peered up at him.

"Nearly three a.m., sweetheart," he said, kissing the top of her head. "Perhaps we should call it a night?"

She gazed up at him dreamily and smiled. "Will we both still be here in the morning?"

"You bet your boots, missy," he said with a grin.

Dan helped her to her feet and walked her to her bedroom.

"Would you like water? A glass of juice? Anything else before heading to bed?"

"I want you!" she said, standing up on tiptoes and smooching his lips.

Dan didn't know whether she was still under the influence of the wine or suffering from pure exhaustion, but he opted not to take advantage of the situation.

"And I want you too, baby," he said fondly, patting her on the rump.

She released a little squeak. "Oh! Do that again!"

Yep. Definitely the wine. Dan should have made sure it was paired with something to eat.

"Not right now, sugar," he said, calmly leading her into her room. "Maybe tomorrow."

"Really?" she said, looking woozy.

"Why don't we get a good night's sleep first?"

"All right," she said as he deposited her inside the threshold.

"Sleep tight, cowgirl," he said, backing away. "See you in the morning."

She bit into her bottom lip and, for the life of him, looked as if she were entertaining very naughty thoughts.

"Is that a promise, Mr. Holbrook?" she said with a giggle.

"That's a promise, Ms. Marsh," he said with a wink.

She lunged forward on her feet and grabbed him by his shirt at his chest, dead-center.

Dan stared down at her in surprise.

"Kiss me good night?" she said, tilting her succulent mouths toward his.

This bit Dan couldn't resist. He was only human.

Dan took her in his arms and gave it to her with everything he had. She was soft and warm and wonderful and, good God almighty, smelled of fresh jasmine blooms. Their mouths blended hungrily, tongues tangling and lips on fire. Her breasts were pressed against him, her hips angling up toward his. Dan released an unintentional groan as he struggled to keep himself under control.

The weight of her collapsed into his arms, and he tightened his grip to hold her.

"Had enough?" he asked, his voice raspy.

In answer, she kissed him again, pressing her fingers under his shirt and up the length of his chest. Heat rushed through him, tightening his thighs and firing his groin. Her hands seized his waist, then slid south, thumbs hitching on either side of his belt. He had to stop this. Dan had to stop this now, or there'd be no turning back.

"Gwen," he said, pushing back. "Wait."

She glanced up at him, eyes questioning.

"Not now, sweetheart. You don't want to do this."

"I don't?" she asked, arching her eyebrows.

Dan stroked her cheek sweetly. "Not here, not like this."

She seemed to collect herself, her face flaming bright red.

"I'm sorry, Dan. I…practically attacked you!"

Dan repressed a smile. "Darling, it's not that I minded. It's just that I want you to be in your right mind when you make your next move. Tonight, you're tired and you've had a little wine. You're not used to drinking at this altitude."

"No," she said, flushing anew, this time from her breastbone to her toes.

"So, tonight we'll rest, okay? Tomorrow we'll have a talk about how we'll plan to get together. How we're going to make this relationship work."

"You're really such a nice man." She whimpered as if she was going to break down bawling.

Dan ran his fingers through his hair, hoping she wouldn't cry, even from tears of joy. He was flat-out exhausted. Plus, he had some serious planning to do.

"Good night, Gwen," he said, pulling shut her bedroom door.

"Good night, Dan," she said shyly, her cheeks and temples aglow.

## Chapter Thirteen

Dan sat on the edge of his bed, knowing he'd done the right thing. As much as he loved Gwen and was desperate to have her, tonight hadn't been the right time. Despite her fiery kisses, she hadn't been ready. In fact, the poor darling had been a wreck. Something had changed between the time he took Rascal down to the barn and had come back here. He guessed she'd been thinking things over and had decided she couldn't go through with it. She'd been as nervous as a filly in a rainstorm when he'd helped her off with her boots. Kissing was all she seemed to want to do, and that was a-okay with him, because he'd come to the advance conclusion they shouldn't let things get too heavy as well.

Then, after a bit of wine and a little nap, she'd turned into this sexy siren who was ready to strip him right there in the hall. But Dan believed it would have been wrong to take advantage of her. He didn't know if that was what she really wanted any more than she did. Dan had sensed the conflict Gwen was facing and had seen it play out firsthand. She wanted to be with him but was afraid, and he understood that. The men in her life she'd mentioned hadn't exactly been the most reliable. First, her father had run out on her, and then her ex-husband had been an absolute jerk. It was no wonder she had mixed feelings about taking this final step in closeness. The people she'd trusted had let her down. Dan understood that when a woman like Gwen slept with a man, trust was of the utmost importance.

While some women thought casual sex was no big deal, and Dan had enjoyed the company of a few of them, he understood that Gwen was of a different ilk. Because of who she was and what she'd been through, he couldn't ask something so intimate and personal of her without granting her assurance they had a future. She was far too vulnerable from her last disaster to take sleeping with a man cavalierly. Dan was trying to remain sensitive to that. He could tell it had helped when he'd told her they would discuss their relationship tomorrow. That was exactly what Dan wanted with Gwen, something long-term that would last beyond her short stay here.

Dan recalled the faint glow on Gwen's cheeks as she'd slipped behind her door, saying good night. It was hard not to imagine her coming to his room instead. In fact, he'd imagined it so hard he'd taken a ten-minute cold shower to dampen those illusions. Dan stared at the wall that separated their rooms, thinking this didn't seem natural. What felt natural was holding Gwen in his arms. It would be natural to love her in an even more complete and physical way. His entire countenance yearned to give itself to Gwen and feel her respond in kind. Dan wanted that more than anything.

Fire welled in his throat as he thought of Gwen going away. He couldn't keep her here forever. Before long, they'd be saying good-bye. Even if they made plans for her return, that still wouldn't stop the pain of separation. Dan felt his chest tighten, sensing how hard that would be. He didn't want Gwen to be two thousand miles across the country from him, damn it. He wanted her here, close enough to hold and talk to. Phone calls, text messages, and video chats couldn't substitute for seeing those beautiful brown eyes in person. Hearing her voice through an electronic device wouldn't take the place of having her beside him and holding his hand, or having her company on a midnight trail ride.

Dan thought of the image he'd had earlier while down at the barn, that picture of the blonde-haired little girl, and his heart stilled. A split second later, it began to beat faster, competing with his racing thoughts. Dan balled his hands into fists, finally understanding what was wrong. He couldn't let Gwen leave Santa Fe without ensuring some kind of commitment between them. Dan had to believe she'd be coming back, and not just for visits either.

Gwen tossed and turned under the covers, not understanding why she couldn't get comfortable. The bed was well appointed enough and plenty roomy. Maybe it was the extra room that was giving her pause. Gwen rolled onto her side and faced the wall that separated her room from Dan's. No doubt he was sound asleep. After his excellent job of playing host and making that fabulous dinner, she could bet he was exhausted. He'd had a full day starting with minding the gallery and ending with a memorable make-out session. Gwen felt her lips pull into a smile, recalling his warmth wrapping around her and his hot and sexy kisses.

Then suddenly, she felt her face burn hot. When Dan had awakened her from her nap, she'd practically thrown herself at him! Nearly pulled his jeans off right outside this door, for heaven's sake. Gwen didn't know what had gotten into her, either the wine or the late-night hour. All she knew was that when he'd walked her back to her room and she'd found herself in his arms, she'd had the inclination to strip him naked. She thought she'd tried it too but couldn't fully recall. That part was fuzzy.

Gwen dropped her face in her hands, vowing to watch her intake of booze during her next visit to New Mexico. She'd been thrilled when Dan had said he wanted a relationship, and hoped that her off-the-charts behavior tonight hadn't changed his mind. Her heart leapt still at the thought that this marvelous feeling would continue. Nothing made her happier than envisioning a future with Dan. She guessed they would work out the logistics in the morning.

Sadness welled within her at the thought of leaving. She knew it was silly to feel down when she had so much to be thankful for. She'd sold her paintings and could help save Marian's house. Her art career had been launched in full as well. On top of all that, she'd met an extraordinary man and had fallen in love with him. What was even more exceptional was that he loved her too. Gwen understood she should be grateful to have met someone as wonderful as Dan. It wasn't ideal that he lived across the country from her, but some people spent a lifetime never finding that special match. It would be hard being apart, but with all the modern technological advances to aid them, they could find their way through. Or could they?

Gwen pulled her pillow to her chest, her heart aching. She wanted to believe so badly things would work out, but was a long-distance affair really what she wanted? One of the things she loved most about Dan was all he had to offer her in person. His warm, caring gaze… That wry twist to his lips… His strong yet tender touch… She supposed she could live without those during the periods when they couldn't see each other, but she didn't know how. Gwen cast her gaze around the darkened room, recalling her earlier projections of a nursery. Already, she'd imagined herself having children with Dan. She knew there were risks involved, but given the advancements in modern medicine, Gwen was sure that she and Dan could arrive at an informed decision. No matter how genetic testing played out, Gwen couldn't imagine any child of hers and Dan's not being an utter blessing.

Gwen startled herself with her calm realization. She didn't just want to date Dan; she wanted a life with him, full-time—right here in New Mexico. There was too much holding him here for Dan to leave Santa Fe. He had roots here and his day job, but more importantly, he ran Paradise Ranch. So many families relied on him, and he was making such a difference to so many kids, Gwen couldn't ask him to walk away.

While she had family commitments in North Carolina, she could arrange for frequent visits. Elizabeth was already well cared for, and Gwen could oversee her finances from a distance. What Elizabeth appreciated most about Gwen was her written communications. It would be easy enough for those to continue. Marian would surely be supportive. She'd want nothing more than for Gwen to be happy, really and truly happy, for the first time in forever. With the tremendous financial burden of meeting her mortgage lifted, Marian would be building a new life for herself anyhow.

Gwen's heart beat faster in hopeful anticipation. Could she dare to believe that Dan might feel the same way? If he did, would he want to take things slowly or charge right ahead like a knight on his steed? She felt her face flush at the memory of that marvelous trail ride. Dan's pronouncements of love had swept her away even more than his kisses. Then later, his steady reserve had told her how greatly he respected her. Dan had sensed she was tipsy, and wasn't going to sleep with her until he believed she had full command of her senses. He cared for her in a thoughtful and selfless way that no man ever had.

She adored him. All that Dan was and stood for were the characteristics she'd sought in a man. Only she hadn't known that until she'd found him. Even in her wildest dreams, she hadn't believed such a phenomenal person existed. Much less could she imagine someone as terrific as that might fall for her. But he had, and now here she was all alone in his guest room on Paradise Ranch. This wasn't the right place for her to stay in this house. She belonged over there with Dan in his arms, lying together with him the whole night through.

Gwen knew she wouldn't sleep a wink tonight with so much running through her heart and head. All she wanted was for the sun to come up so she could spend time with her marvelous man. She couldn't wait to hear what he'd say about their future. Even if he wanted to date for a while and build things between them in a reasonably planned time frame, that was okay by Gwen. All she cared about was that she'd found him and something incredible had begun between them. All good things were worth a wait, and if she had to wait a while longer to have the rest of her dreams come true, she'd be glad to. Gwen was old enough to understand that full-fledged dreams didn't often get handed to you. You had to work at them to bring about your heart's desire. Dan Holbrook was the man she loved and intended to hang on to. She was ready to roll up her sleeves and get cracking. By the time all was said and done, Dan would wholly believe he could never find a woman to love him more completely than Gwen. She was prepared to give him everything she had to offer. She just hoped that was enough.

Dan got up early and went for a morning ride. He had a thing or two he needed to discuss with Rascal, and Rascal was a good one for advice. The best part about him was that he was an excellent listener, encouraging Dan to share his thoughts. Dan led them up the mountain trail to the overlook where he'd taken Gwen last night. The memories of their moonlight kisses heated him like the sun bathing a

cactus flower. God, he loved that woman. He loved her
more than he ever thought possible. Dan hadn't even
known he'd possessed emotions this deep. Now that he'd
admitted it to himself as well as to Gwen, he had to do
something about it.

"What do you think, old boy?" he asked the horse.
"Interested in another filly joining the family?"

Rascal whinnied loudly and stomped one foot.

Dan warmly stroked his mane. "Thought you might
understand."

The horse looked back over his shoulder, giving Dan a
curious snort.

"Well, you've got a girlfriend of your own, don't
you?"

Rascal turned away, pointing his gaze toward the
valley.

"Yep," Dan said, patting his neck. "I figured you'd say
that. It's not all up to me, is it, fellow? My filly has to
agree."

Dan sat there with his horse, staring for a long time as
the sun peeked above the horizon. Paradise Ranch was
Dan's sanctuary, the place he'd always gone to retreat from
the world. Now he could think of nothing better than
having the most beautiful part of that world come and join
him.

If someone had approached Dan two weeks ago and
said he'd be sitting here today having such thoughts, Dan
would have called that person crazy. But that was before
Ms. Gwendolyn Marsh blew into town, upending his heart
like a wild, west wind. By getting to know Gwen, Dan had
come to understand he could never get enough of her.

He'd never forget that first romantic dinner by Loretto
Chapel and the way he'd burned to kiss her. He wanted her
a thousand times more now, and kissing Gwen was only

one of about a million things on his mind. He longed to see that beautiful smile, day after day, until he'd run clear through his final calendar. He wanted to set her free from financial worry and fully support her art. He knew he could build a life with her, one that would make both of them happy.

Dan didn't know how she'd feel about moving to New Mexico, but he wasn't willing to live without her. He had to find a way to make this work.

Gwen awoke to a gorgeous sunrise streaming through the window. She hadn't even realized she'd fallen asleep until the sound of cheery whistling stirred her from her slumber. Dan was in the kitchen banging around with pots and pans. He was also frying bacon, she thought, sensing the heavenly aroma. She sat up happily, feeling her stomach rumble. She hadn't known when she came here that she'd be given the royal treatment. If she had, she wouldn't have thought twice about accepting the invitation. She sprang from the bed, determined to dress quickly and join Dan in the kitchen. Today, they were going to discuss future plans, and she would see the rest of Paradise Ranch. That was something to get up for.

Not ten minutes later, Gwen strolled brightly through the great room, spotting Dan standing by the stove.

"Good morning, sweetheart," he said in a way that made her heart flutter. He flipped flapjacks in a pan, then looked up with a grin. "Hope you're hungry for a big breakfast?"

"Starved," she said eagerly.

Dan motioned to the full pot across the room. "Help yourself to some coffee. Creamer's in the fridge."

"What can I do to help?" she asked, pouring herself a cup.

"You can set the table over there. That would be great."

Gwen found the plates and silverware, then carried them to the cute country table nestled by a big bay window overlooking the valley.

"Everything smells delicious," she said. "I don't know why I'm so ravenous. I could eat a horse!"

Little lines tugged at the edges of his mouth as blue eyes crinkled. "Right, but we won't tell Rascal you said that."

Dan studied her as she buzzed around the kitchen filling juice glasses and folding napkins. She was just too adorable for words, surprisingly domestic-looking too. Didn't matter that she'd apparently put her simple T-shirt on backward. It still fitted her nicely, even with the breast pocket worn in back. He weighed whether he should tell her, then decided not to. If she hadn't figured it out by the time they headed for Santa Fe, he'd drop a subtle hint. In the meantime, there was no real point embarrassing her.

"Have a seat," he said, smiling down at her cowgirl boots. "I wouldn't want you wearing those out before lunchtime."

Gwen laughed, and the musical sound made his heart light. What fun it would be to have her around always. Having breakfast with Gwen day after day would bring Dan nothing but joy. The thought that breakfast would merely be the start of many days that led to long nights in his bed, made Dan even happier. How he hoped she'd say yes.

Dan carried a plate heaping with pancakes over to the table. In his other hand, he carted a platter loaded with bacon and scrambled eggs.

"That's a feast fit for a king," Gwen said, her eyes growing wide.

"We don't have to eat it all, cowgirl," he said with a wink. "Just take what you're hungry for." Dan's appetites at the moment ran far beyond food. He ached to take that beautiful woman in his arms and kiss her good and hard like she deserved and was apparently getting used to.

Gwen's complexion colored from her lovely neck up, as if she'd known what he'd been thinking. If Dan were a betting man, he'd guess she'd been contemplating the same thing, too. Hell, maybe the two of them should just scrap breakfast and get busy loving each other like they were born to do. Dan reined himself in, taking a sip of coffee. One thing at a time, fellow, he told himself. One thing at a time.

"Help yourself," he said. "Best to eat while it's still warm."

Gwen grinned appreciatively, serving enormous portions on her plate. Dan reasoned it was good for her to get her strength up. If everything went as planned, she'd be needing it later.

"Mmm, good," she said, taking a bite of scrambled eggs. "I had no idea what being out in the fresh air would do to me."

"It's great to see you eat healthy. I get so annoyed by those skinny women picking at their food."

Gwen set down her fork in surprise. "Really? I thought men liked skinny women."

"Don't get me wrong," he said teasing a bit. "It's not that I mind them. In fact, it's not so much about size as it is about attitude. I don't care if a woman watches her figure as long as she doesn't make me feel self-conscious at the dinner table. I appreciate women who enjoy their food."

"That's me," she said, raising her hand and taking another bite of bacon. "Mmm. Totally delicious."

Dan chuckled, adoring her. "Yes, it is. That's only one of the many things I love about you."

"Oh?" she said, her cheeks flushed. Amazingly, she stopped chewing a moment. "What's another?"

Dan laughed again. "For one thing, I love that you're so genuine, Gwen. You don't try to be anyone else but yourself. And that's a pretty good thing, because you're one terrific person. You're funny and kind, and a really great listener." He stopped eating as well and pushed his plate aside. "You're also extremely talented and very, very smart. I mean, how couldn't you be? You fell in love with me."

She laughed warmly. "Oh, Dan, you really are the best. Really and truly the best. I feel so lucky to have found you."

"We were fortunate to find each other," he said seriously. "That's why we need to focus on making this work."

"I agree," she said enthusiastically. "We need to take this bull by the horns. Not leave anything to chance."

Dan chuckled in spite of himself. He'd be damned if she wasn't delightful. It was high time he made sure she'd continue to delight him for the rest of his life.

"I agree," he said, leveling her a look. "We should leave nothing to chance, no loopholes or open windows. We need to completely seal this deal."

Dan slid from his chair and crouched on one knee, taking Gwen's hand. Big, brown eyes flashed with surprise as that gorgeous mouth dropped open. She closed it, swallowing hard, her cheeks and temples bright pink. "Dan…" she gasped, her voice a shaky whisper.

"Ms. Gwendolyn Marsh," he said, "from the moment I met you, I knew you were somebody special. I don't know how or why, but I had a definite instinct that you were going to change my life. And boy, have you ever! You've brought me joy and made me laugh. Most important, you've helped me remember what it's like to be in love again." Her face softened into a lovely rainbow as her lips pulled into a smile. "But let me be clear," he continued, "my feelings for you run deeper than any canyon cutting through the New Mexico mountains. I've never, ever had these sorts of feelings for any other woman but you, and I can't bear to lose you. Not for one month, Gwen. Not even for one week or one day. I need you right here beside me, day in and day out, twenty-four/seven. Long distance won't do."

Dan took a deep breath and gazed hopefully in her eyes. "I love you desperately, Gwen. And I want to spend my life with you. Say you'll be my wife?"

Tears streamed down her cheeks as her lovely lips trembled. Gwen squared her small shoulders and gave a saucy tilt to her chin. "Why, Mr. Holbrook," she said. "I thought you'd never ask!"

Dan stood and pulled her into his arms, kissing her soundly. Dan's heart welled with uncontrollable joy. She'd said yes! Gwen was going to be his bride!

"Is there someone back East I should talk to?" he asked, his voice a husky rasp. "Maybe your mom? Marian?"

"I'd like you to meet them both," she said, smiling up at him.

"That can be arranged," he replied with a grin. "How about I fly back with you and we talk to them together?"

She nodded sweetly, transporting him into the heavens.

Dan pressed his forehead to hers and looked lovingly into her eyes. "You sure you'll be okay with moving away and leaving your life as a schoolteacher?"

She caressed him with her gaze, making him feel warm all over.

"The life I want is out here."

"You'll have all the time you need to paint, you know."

"That would be a dream come true."

"Just as long as you leave enough time for that other thing," he said suggestively.

"What other thing?" she asked.

"Getting started on our family," he said, nuzzling her neck.

"Oh Dan…" She seemed to lose her balance, so he steadied his arms around her. "I'd like that. I'd like that very much."

"Of course, I know we'll need to discuss things and work with the doctors. We can go for counseling if you'd like. Talk to some—"

"Dan," she said, stopping him with hot-as-Hades brown eyes. "I want to have your baby."

She gave him a sensuous kiss, pressing her jalapeño-pepper-hot body up against his until Dan thought he might explode from the sheer torture.

"How soon can we get started?" he asked, his tone urgent with desire.

Gwen saucily tilted her head to one side and cocked an eyebrow. "Want to help me off with these boots?"

Dan loved this woman more than he'd ever loved anybody on the planet. He thanked his lucky stars that he was finally getting an opportunity to show her.

"That, Ms. Marsh," he said, with a warm, willing grin, "would be my great pleasure."

Then, with one powerful motion that he'd mentally practiced two dozen times, Dan swept his sexy cowgirl off her feet and carried her to his bed.

# Epilogue

The sun angled high in the summer sky, casting a cheery glow across the Sangre de Cristo Mountains. In the riding ring behind the barn, Gwen helped a young boy with an unsteady gait mount Rascal.

"Are you sure he'll be all right?" his coed aide asked with concern.

"Oh yes," Gwen said, smiling brightly. "I'll be with him the whole time. Besides," she said, gently stroking the horse, "old Rascal's a real softie."

Rascal snorted loudly and stomped his foot as Dan led a lovely palomino into the ring.

Dan grinned and winked at Gwen. "Sounds like old Rascal's been missing his honey."

Gwen laughed as one of their trained riders approached to help a slight child up on the mare. "We'll be back in an hour," she told Dan once the other pair had settled in.

Dan set his hands on his hips, proudly surveying the scene. Gwen delighted in the sight of him, more at home now than he'd ever been on this ranch.

"Oh, I nearly forgot to tell you," he said. "Nancy called this morning. She sold another landscape series. The ones including the horse."

Gwen beamed from ear to ear. "Why, thanks, Rascal," she said, nuzzling his nose and giving it a kiss. Rascal nibbled lightly on her curls, tickling her ear. "Who knew you'd be such a great model"

The palomino protested loudly, scraping the dirt with her hoof.

"Of course you did," Dan told her with a laugh.

Just then, a small girl with springy yellow curls rushed into the ring.

"Daddy! Daddy!" she called, racing toward Dan. "Guess what I got!"

Dan smiled kindly and scooped her into his arms. "What's that, pumpkin?"

The child happily waved a report card. "An A in music!" she proclaimed with glee. "The teacher says I'm the best student she's got!"

"I think that's wonderful, honey," Gwen said, mounting Rascal behind her small charge.

Dan kissed his little daughter. "Yes, sweetheart, really terrific."

Gwen gave Rascal a loud command, then paraded past Dan, wearing her favorite pair of boots. Catching his gaze, she squared her small shoulders and gave a saucy tilt to her chin.

"Who do you think taught her to sing?"

Little lines pulled at the edges of his mouth as blue eyes crinkled.

"Hurry home, cowgirl," Dan said. "We'll be waiting for you."

## The End

# A Note from the Author

Thanks for reading *Santa Fe Fortune.* I hope you enjoyed it. If you did, please help other people find this book.

1. This book is lendable, so loan it to a friend who you think might like it so that she (or he) can discover me, too.

2. Help other people find this book: write a review.

3. Sign up for my newsletter so that that you can learn about the next book as soon as it's available. Write to GinnyBairdRomance@gmail.com with "newsletter" in the subject heading.

4. Visit my website for details on other books available now: http://www.GinnyBairdRomance.com.

## Also By Ginny Baird

*The Sometime Bride*
*Real Romance*
*How to Marry a Matador*
*The Christmas Catch*
*The Holiday Bride*

To see an excerpt from *How to Marry a Matador,* keep reading for a sneak peek here!

## HOW TO MARRY A MATADOR

*Fernando sighed, worry lines creasing his brow. "You're terribly angry with me, aren't you?"*

*"It takes two to tango, Fernando. I'm not saying all of this is your fault. I played a part in what happened yesterday too."*

*He turned toward her with a penetrating look. "That's what I don't understand. Why did you?"*

*Jess felt a lurch of emotion as he dissected her with his earnest green gaze. "I...don't know."*

*He leaned toward her with a husky whisper. "Oh, but I think you do."*

*He drew nearer, his mouth hovering over hers. Jess cursed herself for so badly wanting his kiss. His kisses had been so tantalizing last night, they'd made her lose all sense of reason. And it wasn't just the way he'd held her. When he'd looked deep in her eyes and said that one thing, she'd inexplicably believed him as she had no man before.*

*"Why did you?"*

*Fernando reached out and cupped her chin in his hand. "Because, querida, when I saw you standing there in that garden, with that beautiful smile on your lips, I knew with a certainty that I'd have to claim them. That I wouldn't rest until I made you mine."*

*"It was a simple sexual attraction."*

*"There was nothing simple about it," he said, brushing his lips to hers.*

*Jess closed her eyes as her heart stilled. She couldn't let herself do this, but she couldn't stop herself either. His masculine scent washed over her as she felt his palm press into the small of her back.*

*"Jessica," he said, resting his forehead on hers. "When I tell you the truth about this morning, I don't want you to believe that anything last night was a lie." And then to prove it, he kissed her deeply, with a skill and a passion that made her lose grip of her wine, sending the contents of her cup sloshing sideways.*

*"Your sister's riding pants," she said, nearly breathless.*

*"They'll wash," he said, tenderly stroking her thigh.*

*"Fernando," Jess gasped, pulling back. "We can't."*

*He studied her a thoughtful moment as she gazed at him wide-eyed.*

*"Then we won't," he said with a quick peck on her lips.*

*She shivered involuntarily in spite of herself. This man had a way of completely undoing her.*

*"We'll have a little something to eat first." He pulled several small bundles from his bag, along with a small knife and a cutting board.*

*"While we talk?"*

*"Of course," he said, handing her a napkin for her slacks. "Then afterwards, I'll let you decide."*

*"Decide what?"*

*Fernando shot her a sexy grin as he refilled her wine.*

*"Whether or not I'm the husband of your dreams."*

# Chapter One

Jess rolled over into a wall of steel. She opened her eyes, encountering a strong, masculine shoulder. Hoofbeats echoed outside to the sound of *ándale, ándale, vámanos*! Her gaze panned the spread of his broad, olive chest, graced with charcoal hair matching the wavy array on his head. Impossibly perfect cheekbones offset a patrician nose. No Renaissance sculptor could have crafted a finer face. Jess's mind whirled, recalling the evening of wild flamenco dancing and sangria. *This slumbering specimen can't be, but he is!*

She gingerly lifted the sheet and peered beneath it with a gasp.

"Good morning, *princesa*," he said, emerald eyes upon her.

Jess pinched the duvet to her chest, her face on fire. "Fernando."

He turned toward her, covers gaping. "I trust you slept well," he said, trailing a finger down her arm. Little shivers raced up her spine, then plummeted in a dead heat toward her tailbone. He brought warm lips to her shoulder, gracing it with a kiss. "I also hope," he said, his Spanish accent trilling, "you meant what you said last night."

Panic tore through her as she desperately tried to recall. Gracefully, he filled in the blank. "That you were happy to be my wife." *Wife? Did he just say wife?*

Fernando tenderly peeled back the duvet, admiring the curve of her hip beneath a satiny sheer nighty. His palm centered on the small of her back as he angled his ruggedly handsome face toward hers. "And you took pains to prove it," he said in a husky rasp, pressing her lower region toward his vivid response.

Jess pushed back with a start and pinched her forearm, certain she would wake up. He lazily pulled himself partially upright on one elbow, resting his head in his hand.

Jess stared, dumbfounded, while Fernando lifted his brow and waited.

"What...is the meaning of this?" she asked, covering herself primly.

"Don Fernando!" a voice called through the screenless window in gruff Castilian. "You still riding this morning?"

Fernando shot Jess a questioning look. She quickly shook her head.

"Not today, Pedrito!" he called back in English. "We're sorry to have troubled you!"

"We?" Jess asked, her voice escaping as a whisper.

"You insisted I take you riding. Don't you recall? It was the second thing you wished to do as my new wife."

Jess felt the heat bolt to her temples and chin. Suddenly, it all came back to her. The late night at the bodega, Fernando's unexpected and utterly passionate kiss, their unanticipated encounter with that Catholic priest... Jess swallowed hard past the burn in her throat.

She'd come to Madrid on an acquisitions merger but had married a matador instead.

Fernando watched as the beautiful woman leapt from the bed, snatching the duvet with her. Honey-blonde hair cascaded past delicate shoulders as she suddenly averted brilliant blue eyes. "You should cover yourself," she insisted.

"But it seems my new wife has taken the covers."

"And stop saying that!" she cried with an indignant pout.

"What? That you're my wife? I do apologize," he said, sitting upright and scooting to the edge of the bed. "Perhaps it's better if I call you my bride."

Jess instinctively stepped back. "Now, Fernando," she began with a wave of her finger. "You know as well as I do that—if anything happened last night—it wasn't supposed to."

He noticed she was trying not to peek at him but was failing in her efforts. He took this as encouragement to drop his feet to the floor and face her outright, sporting his full glory.

"Is that what you Americans mean by, *Take me back to your bed, you beast. I'm yours?*"

She gasped audibly. "I said that?" she asked with unmasked horror.

Taking pity on the woman, Fernando covered his lap with a feather pillow. "You can look now," he said with a sigh.

She steadied her chin, settling her gaze on the window. "How do I know I can trust you?"

"I guess you don't," he replied. "But I'm inviting you to take the chance."

Slowly, she turned her eyes toward his. They were an amazing shade of blue, aquamarine, really. Fernando felt as if he could swim in them forever. He recalled thinking that yesterday evening, after a few too many pitchers of sangria and a splendidly expensive bottle of cava. Perhaps he'd gotten carried away in asking her to be his bride. But after the flamenco show and the kiss by the fountain, their surprise encounter with his old friend Father Domingo had seemed nothing less than a direct sign from God.

"Where are my clothes?" she asked, color sweeping the bridge of her nose.

Fernando pointed to the armoire beside the door leading to the well-appointed bathroom.

"I suppose the shower's in there?" she asked, angling her head in that direction.

"There are fresh towels on the stand behind the claw-foot tub," he said.

Her cheeks flamed red. Perhaps she did remember everything.

"Fine, thank you," she said hoarsely, sidestepping her way across the floor, the hem of the duvet trailing over inlaid tile.

"Would you like something to eat?" he called after her. "I can have Consuelo bring up breakfast."

She skittered into the bathroom, partially closing the door. "Just coffee!" she called before shutting it with a bang.

Fernando sat upright with a start and tossed aside the pillow.

"Consuelo?" he said into the intercom by the bed, pressing its button.

"*¿Sí, señor?*" a kindly older voice asked from the kitchen.

"*Dos café con leche, por favor.*"

"*Two*, Don Fernando?"

While it had come as surprise, Fernando didn't precisely view his marriage as a mistake. In fact, given the timeline imposed by his grandfather for inheriting his fortune, this little twist of fate just might prove fortuitous.

"*Sí, dos.* And, if you will, place a pretty, fresh rose on the tray. I have something happy to tell you."


Jess let the water run hot, hitting her full in the face. Any second now, she was going to wake up in her apartment in Brooklyn, her best friend Evie calling her on the phone about some recent catastrophe that had occurred... Jess's mind raced, putting pieces of the puzzle together.

Fernando Garcia de la Vega's emerging telecommunications firm had been a long-term associate of her multinational corporation headquartered in New York. While Jess wasn't super tech-savvy, she knew how money worked. Trained in the banking industry, she'd earned her stripes by helping arrange the takeover of United National Savings & Loan's domestic division by InTrust Corp. While she'd really been the second in that job, her magnanimous superior had given her the bulk of the credit. The offer to head up the foreign acquisitions office at Global Financial Telecom had come just two weeks later. She'd accepted the post with a mixture of joy and trepidation. There she was at twenty-eight, and—according to everyone else—finally making her way. Inwardly, she feared she'd bitten off more than she could chew. She'd never handled such a large responsibility alone. What if she made a disaster of it all and failed everybody in the process?

While Global Financial had started as a bank, it quickly expanded into the lucrative computing field, piloting the first purse-size, all-purpose computer. With computing and telecommunications becoming so intricately linked, interest in other types of personal electronic devices followed. So far, Jess had done a reasonable job, impressing her stern, middle-aged boss Madeline with her string of unlikely successes. She didn't know how her mergers had always come through, but it appeared as if she had an invisible good luck charm buried somewhere deep in her pocket. Each time she got assigned to something new, Jess silently feared her luck would run out. Now, it appeared it finally had.

Jess shut off the water and reached for a towel, her gaze panning toward the bedroom. How could she have let herself get swept away? So what if Fernando was gorgeous, intelligent, and had an accent to die for? That was no reason to go shedding her clothes and getting married! Jess cinched the towel around herself, realizing she had that in the wrong order. The marriage part had come before the hopping into bed. But why had she done it? She wasn't that old-fashioned, for heaven's sake. Sleeping with a man after a few too many sangrias and a momentary lapse in judgment was one thing. Saying "I do" under the arch of an orange tree in the courtyard of some small church whose name she couldn't pronounce was something else entirely.

Jess warmed at the memory of Fernando kissing her by the main plaza's fountain, sweetly at first—and then with the passion of a parched man determined to drink her in. Her face flashed hot as she further recalled Fernando's skilled, masculine touch once he'd brought her back to his lair. The ranch was breathtaking in its desolate beauty, rows of olive trees threaded by moonlight, a faraway vineyard trailing over burnt hills.

She hadn't even known he'd come from a family of matadors or had once worked as a bullfighter himself. These were stories he told to few people, he'd assured her with a tender caress before leading her up the stairs. While the townsfolk of La Esperanza del Corazón viewed him as a hero, in Madrid Fernando was just a successful businessman. Neither the family he came from nor the world he'd left behind had any bearing on his corporate potential. So he'd shuttered away his past, vowing to reserve its unveiling only for those special parties with whom he might share a future. He'd led her to his bed then, saying that their impromptu marriage had been a blessing, something he'd never wish undone—no matter how she might think of him tomorrow. And, when he'd offered to show her the scar that tore from his upper left thigh to his navel, she'd found it impossible to say no.

Jess moistened a washcloth from a nearby stand with cool water and pressed it to her chest. Fine trickles slid south, gliding into her cleavage.

Okay, so she'd admit it. Ever since they'd first met six months ago, she'd been reduced to a handful of putty each time he'd given her that deep, expressive look with those impossibly unnerving eyes. Still, she'd steeled herself against him, understanding that when he was being flirty, it was likely in the interest of his own financial gain. That was just what Fernando was: untrustworthy. Which was precisely why she had no reason to trust him now. Fernando was up to something with this marriage bit, and Jess was determined to learn what. But first, she needed to find an Internet connection and research Spanish marriage laws. Surely, things couldn't be as bad as they seemed.

Fernando hummed a love song and strategically angled the tray, rearranging its bud vase for maybe the tenth time. *Ridiculous*, he told himself. It was only a flower. But none could be as sweet as the delicate rose that had opened up for him last night. Fernando would be a liar to say he hadn't wanted her—*ached for her*—for months on end. He'd never seen a face so lovely or known a mind so sharp. Hers was such an intoxicating combination, he might even have married her without the wine.

Though he'd secretly imagined laying her in his bed at least a dozen times, he'd never envisioned the sheer ecstasy of actually being with her. She was so sweet yet tough, like a tiger in the wild. And her kisses were the nearest thing to heaven. If the bright Andalusian sun hadn't awakened him from his slumber, he might have thought he'd fantasized the whole thing. He'd stirred early to find a sleeping angel beside him, then had quickly shut his eyes, lest she evaporate like an enchanted dream. The next thing he knew, she was moving beside him, carefully peering under the sheet to ensure he possessed the correct…accoutrements needed to fulfill his husbandly duties. Fernando sighed, thinking he'd be glad to perform those again and at any time his willing wife was ready.

He stared toward the bathroom, noting the shower had stopped. This might not be the most standard way to begin a union, but it certainly couldn't be the worst. Fernando was sure that Jessica would agree—once she got over the shock.

Jess exited the bathroom with a combative air and made a beeline for the armoire.

"Coffee this morning?" he asked, smiling sweetly over the rim of a cup. He extended it in her direction with the calm demeanor of a waiter at an upscale restaurant. She noted his lower region was still covered by a large feather pillow, the musculature of his tanned upper thighs exposed to the morning breeze fluttering in through the window. His toned olive chest sported richly dark hair which tapered in perfect symmetry down the line of his taut abs and plummeted toward the breakfast tray balanced on his lap.

She hesitated a moment, then decided she'd think better after the java. "Fernando," she said, cinching the oversized towel around her and cautiously inching forward. "You and I have something to discuss."

He handed her the coffee, then nonchalantly dipped a bit of pastry in his own cup. "I never discuss business before breakfast," he said, slurping loudly. "Mmm. This *pan dulce* is delicious. You ought to try it."

"I'm not hungry," she said, steadying the cup in her hands.

"Ah yes, that's right," he replied with a knowing wave of his finger. "Fairly well satisfied last night. Eh?"

Jess felt her face flash hot as his impish green eyes danced with mirth. "I don't find any of this very amusing."

"I'm sorry, Jessica," he said sadly. "I suppose I was a fool, hoping that you'd be just as excited about this as I."

She took a slow sip of coffee, studying him all the while. "You claim to be a fool, Fernando. But you're certainly not fooling me."

He raised his brow, perplexed.

"Come on," she said. "Give. What's in this for you?"

"My new wife has cut me to the quick," he said, bringing a hand to his chest.

"Argh!" She spun toward the armoire, clumsily setting down her cup down on a nearby stand. Porcelain clattered against itself with the effort.

"You're getting too upset about this," he said.

"I...don't...think...so," she said as she furiously tugged her clothes from huge wooden hangers, then strode toward the bathroom.

"*Querida,*" Fernando said softly, "please wait."

She stopped walking, her pulse pounding. It picked up as she felt him behind her, his warmth drawing near. Instinct said that Fernando hadn't carried the pillow—or anything else—with him. "Perhaps it was…impetuous, unexpected," he said, palms pressed to her bare upper arms. Goose bumps rose on her flesh as the heat of his breath warmed her neck. "But you can't completely believe it was wrong."

But it was wrong, worse than wrong. Marrying Fernando had to be the most terrible decision she'd ever made!

"I have a boyfriend," she said, the lie escaping as a whisper.

"What a shame." Palms slid down her arms as Fernando brought his lips to her shoulder. "How do you think he'll take the news?"

Jess gasped, fighting her automatic feminine response. Nipples hardened beneath terrycloth, and she ached to turn toward him. Being made love to by a strong, confident man like Fernando was nothing short of heaven. The truth was that she and Allen had broken up weeks ago, and the physical relationship they'd shared hadn't even come close. Still, the illusion of another man was good, maybe the best thing she had at the moment. Until her head cleared, Jess needed every ounce of ammunition against Fernando's manly advances that she could muster.

"He'll be outraged," she said, pulling her mound of clothing in tighter.

"He must love you desperately."

Jess pursed her lips, fighting the fire in her eyes. The fact was, she didn't know whether Allen had loved her or not. Just as with her past two boyfriends, he'd never broached the topic—and she'd never yearned to discuss it.

"I don't do love," she said hoarsely, making an effort to step away.

Fernando tightened his grip and spun her toward him. "Everybody *does* love," he said with an earnest look. "Sooner or later."

Jess blinked back the moisture in her eyes. "Not this girl."

Fernando released her, his brow creasing. He'd never seen a woman at once so fragile and strong. There was a sorrow in her eyes that made him want to weep for, and with, her. He wondered how long she'd contained it, keeping that sadness to herself.

"I'll just be a minute," she said, turning away.

Fernando watched her leave, thinking this presented more of a challenge than he'd imagined. Then again, if ever there was a man who knew how to rise to the occasion, it was him.

"Take all the time that you need," he said as she exited the room.

Jessica emerged fully dressed ten minutes later. "As soon as we return to Madrid," she said, "we're getting this thing annulled." She was beautiful today, smartly polished in a short white dress. He'd be proud to introduce her, if only she'd trade that frown on her lips for one of those winning smiles.

"Annulled?" Fernando questioned, glancing sideways as he straightened the collar of his polo shirt in the mirror. "Don't you think that's a little rash?"

"No, Fernando. Rash is getting married to a business colleague after too much sangria. Rash is *not* doing the sensible thing the next morning."

Jess didn't know how she'd let herself get talked into it, but she had. Right down to signing that statement of Proof of Freedom to Marry, endorsed by Father Domingo's brother-in-law, the retired American Consul, whose powers of persuasion were still apparently in force.

"But we weren't married in Madrid," he noted astutely.

Jess considered this a moment, realizing he was right. The marriage had to be annulled right here. But first, she needed to learn precisely where that was. "Where are we?"

"In La Esperanza del Corazón, remember? Place of my birth."

Yes, it all came stampeding back to her, like a trillion *toros* on the run. "Of course I recall."

"Everything...?" he asked, suggestively lifting an eyebrow.

Jess shook her head in agitation. She was not going to let him do this, have her remembering all the *wrong* things. "I was tipsy...animated, okay? Foolishly and hopelessly in love with life!"

He beheld her wistfully. "Yes, it was lovely."

Jess fought for the words. "It was reckless," she countered. "That woman you were with last night wasn't me."

"No? Who was it?"

"Someone else." She huffed, trying to imagine how she'd explain this to her mother. Jess had never gotten so much as a B on a report card. Now here she was, failing life. "My evil twin."

He laughed out loud. "You're a Gemini?"

"What?"

"The zodiac sign."

She was puzzled by this turn in the conversation.

"What do constellations have to do with anything?"

"Perhaps we're written in the stars," he said, a sly smile on his lips.

Jess pressed her palms to her temples, thinking hard. Before she told her mother, she'd call Evie; that was what she'd do. Evie would help her straighten things out. If Jess could fix things fast, maybe her mom wouldn't even have to know.

"I'm a Taurus, if it matters."

"I might have guessed."

"What's that's supposed to mean?"

"The Taurus and the toreador? And you tell me there's no fate?"

She set her jaw, her eyes boring into his. "Fernando Garcia de la Vega, I want you to show me to an Internet connection this minute!"

"That might be a bit complicated. You see, out here *en el campo*, we have limited..." His voice fell off as he took in her increasingly enraged form. It was one thing to lightheartedly provoke someone. But at this very moment, Fernando sensed he was putting himself in mortal danger. "Okay, all right," he said, flagging a hand in her direction. "I can see when I'm not wanted."

His expression took a downcast turn that almost made her feel sorry for him. The truth was, Jess had wanted him, *wanted him in the worst way*, which was precisely what had gotten her into this mess! She pulled her cell from her purse and checked it for the tenth time this morning. She still wasn't picking up service. Just how far from civilization were they?

Fernando gestured grandly toward the door that led downstairs. He unlocked it, then held it open. "Fair's fair, Jessica. After all, no one's holding you prisoner in an ivory tower. So, here's what we'll do. You and I will have a civilized talk about everything that happened last night.

Then, if you're still determined to get out of this marriage, I won't stop you. I'm far too proud a man to hold a woman against her will."

Jess's heart skipped a beat as something raw and unanticipated burned inside her. She couldn't say whether it was relief she felt or something more akin to disappointment. Why, oh why did his admission that he was fine in letting her go resonate with something so utterly painful in her core?

Jess shook off the odd déjà vu and met his gaze, his green eyes playing the soft serenade of a Spanish guitar. Jess caught her breath, lost for a moment in their music.

"I also believe," he said slowly, "that sometimes things happen for a reason. And often that reason is far too grand for us to originally understand."

But Jess didn't want to think about reasons or fate or star-crossed lovers—or any of that other nonsense Evie so ardently believed in but that she'd never been able to wrap her own head around. Jess was a practical person who saw the world for what it was. The fact that she'd long ago stopped believing in fairy tales had only worked to her benefit.

"The only thing I need to understand," she said, "is why you persist in saying this…accident of nature…was somehow preordained. "

He massaged his temples, apparently growing exasperated. "I already said I'll explain everything."

"Good," she said, stepping past him. "At last, you're talking sensibly."

Jess hurried down the stairs, desperate to get away. He smelled of sandalwood soap and lime, and the aroma awakened her memory of his showering kisses last night. The sooner she got herself out of this mistake of an arrangement, the better. And it better be before nightfall, lest she find herself tempted to leap back into that manly matador's bed.

"I've never been accused of being unreasonable," he said, trailing after her. "But I am known for keeping my commitments."

Jess halted in her tracks, fearing this was going somewhere. Somewhere that was going to land dangerously close to further confounding her emotions.

He captured her in his gaze, stilling her heart for a fraction of a second. Somehow, when he looked at her, it was as if he could see into her depths and behold her every weakness. And yet, his gaze soothed her, smoothing old hurts in tender ways. Warmth surged in her cheeks as he descended the steps two at a time, then gently cupped her face in his hands.

"And I *always* honor my commitments," he said, his voice a husky rasp.

Her pulse beat wildly, and for a second, she feared he would kiss her. Next, she was terribly afraid he might not.

"Most especially," he continued with an enigmatic smile, "to my mother."

# Chapter Two

Jess couldn't believe she was having lunch with Fernando's mother. Everything was totally out of control. Señora Garcia de la Vega took a slow sip of wine, surveying the American seated before her. "Tell me again, dear," she asked, the sweetness of her tone slightly acerbic, "how is it that you know my Fernando?"

Fernando dabbed his mouth with a napkin, then set the cloth aside. "We met in Madrid. I explained the whole thing to you this morning."

"Perhaps," his mother said with a tilt of her chin. "But I'd like to hear the story from the young lady herself."

That would be great, if only Jess could recall the tale she was supposed to tell. She had no clue what Fernando had said to his mother earlier. All she knew was that Fernando had asked her to *"play along with things at lunch."* He promised her an Internet connection later, along with a cell signal in range so she could call Evie. Boy, would Evie have a field day with this. She was forever on Jess's case for being too stringent and unerring. Eve was the carefree one who made mistakes. Now, here Jess sat in the middle of some matador's ranch—and the global communications magnate didn't even have Wi-Fi! Things were positively prehistoric in La Esperanza del Corazón, and Jess had the feeling she was dining with a carnivore.

Mrs. Garcia de la Vega's deep brown eyes settled on hers as she carefully spooned cold gazpacho soup to her lips. Fernando's mother had to be in her late fifties but was beautiful still, fine wisps of gray just making themselves visible in her coiled-up hair.

Fernando reached across the table and squeezed Jess's hand, lending encouragement. "Just tell her how we met, *querida.* All the business deals and such." He lifted her hand to give the back of it a firm kiss, and Jess's resolve wilted. She was not seriously interested in Fernando in the least. They had chemistry—nothing more. And she resented the trappings of this little charade confusing her.

Jess withdrew her hand from his grip and massaged it with the one in her lap. "Yes, that's right," she politely told Mrs. Garcia de la Vega. "It was business. All business. Strictly business from the start." She shot Fernando a stern look to remind him their business here was nearly done.

"And your business is…?" the older woman prompted.

"Telecommunications, just like mine," Fernando interjected.

"The young woman speaks just fine for herself," his mother quipped, annoyed.

Jess uncrossed her legs under the table and sat up a little straighter in her chair.

"The name of my firm is Global Financial Telecom. We're headquartered in New York, and I'm in charge of international acquisitions."

"Like my son, for example," Señora Garcia de la Vega said flatly.

A breeze ruffled across the tabletop, sending the fresh-flower centerpiece fluttering. While Jess normally loved dining outdoors, the chill hovering above them on this balmy afternoon was unmistakable.

"I came here on an acquisitions merger, it's true. Involving your son's *company*, Señora Garcia de la Vega. Fernando knew about… What I mean is, this was all arranged in advance. There were no surprises."

"Except for one," Fernando added with a wink.

A tension in her gut told her she was about to get broadsided. "Which one was that?"

"Why, you know, my love. That little unexpected package."

Jess felt the blood drain from her face. "Package?"

"Special delivery, *mi amor*. Our bundle of joy." Fernando scooted his chair against hers so he could drape his arm around her shoulder. "Mamá," he said, addressing his mother sincerely. "Jessica and I have known each other for months now. I've come to respect her not just as a business colleague but as a woman as well. A beautiful, sensuous woman that any man would be proud to call—"

"Is there a restroom downstairs?" Jess asked, abruptly pushing back from the table and breaking Fernando's embrace. She stood unsteadily, glancing helplessly about the patio. Oddly, she felt more trapped in this beautifully arranged open space than in any cage.

"Past the kitchen," Mrs. Garcia de la Vega stated, her quizzical gaze on her son.

Fernando shrugged at his mom as Jess stood from her chair. "It's the baby."

"*Baby?*" The joint chorus was so loud neither Jess nor Mrs. Garcia de la Vega could be sure whose shriek registered the loudest.

Jess stared at Fernando and blinked hard, her wobbling knees forcing her back in her chair. "*That's too high a telecommunications price tag,*" she hissed under her breath.

"Consuelo!" Señora Garcia de la Vega cried desperately toward the house. "More water, please!"

Jess didn't know what game Fernando was playing, but she refused to be party to it. "Excuse me," she said, gathering her strength and standing again. "Mrs. Garcia de

la Vega, thanks for a lovely meal, but it's time I head back
to Madrid."

"Madrid?" Fernando and his mother parroted together.

"Yes, Fernando. Madrid. That's where I have an
apartment—with an included Internet connection."

Mrs. Garcia de la Vega set aside her empty water
glass. "We have an Internet connection."

Jess raised an accusatory eyebrow at Fernando.
"Here?"

"Naturally," his mother continued. "Premium satellite.
What else would you expect?"

What else would she expect, indeed? Nothing more
than Fernando's continued conniving. The man didn't have
an honest bone in his body!

"But Jessica," he began, pleading, "our arrangements.
You and I should talk…alone."

"I think that's a very good idea," his mother said
grimly. "This situation sounds serious. It is not one you
settle in haste."

Fernando stood with a gallant air and took her by the
elbow. "This way, *querida*. We wouldn't want a woman in
your condition taxing her nerves." Then he called back over
his shoulder, "I'll see to it she calms down, Mamá."

As viciously as she could, Jess stomped her three-inch
heel into Fernando's loafer.

"Ouch!"

"Son?" Mrs. Garcia de la Vega inquired as they
slipped out the door.

"It's nothing. I just felt a sudden…twinge," he said,
leading Jess from the room.

"Of guilt, I hope," Jess spewed under her breath.

"All right, Fernando," Jess whispered as Consuelo whisked by them, carting a chilled bottle of water. "What precisely was going on in there?"

Fernando raked his fingers through his hair, then addressed her with a strained expression. "The truth?"

"That would be a nice start."

"Okay, I'll tell you, but not here."

"Not here? Then where?"

Consuelo passed back by them, and Fernando called after her. "Consuelo, if you please, ask Don Pedrito to saddle up two horses."

Jess stared at him aghast. "First I'm pregnant; next I'm riding?"

"My mother rode until she was full term."

"Oh! That's what happened to you! Too many prenatal bumps to the noggin!"

"You *can* ride?" he asked.

She set her hand on her hip. "I was raised in a saddle."

"That settles it."

"*Gracias*, Consuelo," he said to the housekeeper, who studied them agape. Consuelo backed away, clearly not wanting to miss one moment of the action.

"What's all the shouting about?" Señora Garcia de la Vega called from outside.

Fernando pressed his palms together in a prayer position. "Please, dear Jessica, I'm begging you—for only a few more hours of your time. The rest of your life... whatever you opt to do with the information... those choices are yours."

Mrs. Garcia de la Vega stood in her spacious kitchen sternly appraising her son. "Are you sure you should take a woman in her condition riding? She's an American, you know, on the soft side."

"She's as healthy as a horse. Kickboxes, even. I'm sure she'll be fine."

"Kicks boxes, eh?" his mother asked. "And then what will she beat up next? Your heart, more than likely."

"No, Mamá, you misunderstand. It's an exercise."

His mother frowned, fine lines creasing her brow.

"Well, I hope she leaves kicking behind once she's a mother. It doesn't sound dignified and surely won't prove any sort of example—"

He fondly patted his mother's cheek. "I'll put her on Valencia, okay? She's as gentle as a lamb, and too old to trot too fast."

"We need to talk about this, Fernando. In detail."

"I know," he said, briefly holding her gaze, "but not yet."

"This has all happened so quickly. I didn't even know you were dating!"

"We more or less skipped over that part."

Señora Garcia de la Vega inhaled a sharp breath and narrowed her gaze. "Does this have something to do with your birthday?" She leaned into the center island as Fernando packed libations for his trip. Some noncarbonated water and a bottle of a regional Rioja. Almost as an afterthought, he tucked a wedge of Manchego cheese and a small hard roll in his satchel.

"I'm sorry," he asked blithely, "did you say something?"

She stood with her arms akimbo, lording over her kitchen. The moment Consuelo had sensed the ensuing fireworks, she'd made herself scarce.

Señora Garcia de la Vega disapprovingly shook her head. "You're forgetting the almonds. And, oh yes, the olives."

"*Gracias.* They slipped my mind."

She huffed as he stuffed small portions of these in his bag as well.

"So?" she asked. "Are you going on a picnic or running away?"

Since he'd been eight years old, the latter had crossed Fernando's mind more than a dozen times. Yet he would never leave her. When his father had died at forty-nine, Fernando had been left manning the ranch. While he'd grown older and had moved to Madrid, his heart remained in La Esperanza del Corazón. He would always take care of his mother. She'd been his source of strength and had granted him the freedom to follow his dreams, even when they included—for a time—dabbling in the one profession she'd prayed to God he'd never pursue.

"We won't be gone long," he said, buttoning up his satchel. "Back by nightfall, *vale*?"

She paused for a thoughtful moment, seeming to soften just a little. "Fernando," she said, "are you sure you're doing the right thing? Is this girl really the one?"

He pensively eyed his mother, knowing she wished only to protect him.

"The situation is…complicated," he said truthfully, without giving too much away.

"Love is always complicated," she admitted with resignation in her eyes.

"Yes, Mamá," he said, kissing her on the forehead. "It is."

"I still don't think this is a good idea for the baby!" she called after him. "I was an experienced horsewoman, you know!"

He turned back with a gentle smile. "If she shows any signs of trouble, we'll abandon the horses immediately. Jessica's in top form, and it's still very early. I can assure you with my word as your son, I would never take my new bride riding if I felt that our child was in danger."

# Chapter Three

Jess gripped the satellite phone with white knuckles. "He's a liar and a cheat, and I don't know *how* I let myself get talked into this!"

Evie's calm voice resonated from the other side of the Atlantic. "Now, if you'd just take a deep breath and calm down, maybe I'd be able to understand you. Inhale, come on."

Jess imagined Evie was twisting up her hair, as she did when taking on her consultant role. Evie's fiery red tresses fell in ringlets to her shoulders. She had a habit of twisting them into a French knot and securing it with any handy implement. Even a chopstick or a pencil would do. Jess had always envied that ability, as her own stick-straight hair wouldn't even hold a barrette.

Jess took a deep breath, then let it out slowly.

"Better?"

"Are we on speakerphone?" Jess asked.

"Nobody's here. Out for the three-martini lunch." Evie worked in a small yet prestigious publishing firm where publicity deals were forever being cut. As an assistant, she practically ran the place but still barely got paid. Jess was secretly ashamed to earn so much more than her, knowing that Evie worked just as hard. Jess didn't feel nearly as smart or savvy as everyone thought she was. She owed her early success to a series of lucky breaks. If things had broken differently, it could just as easily have been her sitting in her old college roommate's chair.

"Well, I'd appreciate you taking it off, just the same."

Evie's reply came back without the previous echo effect. "Okay, so tell me again, because I know I didn't hear you clearly. It sounded almost like you'd said you'd gotten married!" She affected a laugh.

Jess's heart lurched in her chest. It *did* sound absurd, and she knew it. Especially for her. Jess winced, hearing her voice come out as a squeak. "It's true, Evie. Oh my God."

"*What?*"

Jess bit into her knuckle, stopping her knee-jerk reaction at the first flash of pain. Her pulse was racing, and her head pounded. As bad this already was, somehow it sounded worse admitting it to her best friend. "I did it, Evie. Just last night. I married a matador."

Evie's tone was shrill with disbelief. "How did you do that?"

Jess grimaced. "It was a mistake."

Evie huffed into her mouthpiece. "No, Jess, a *mistake* is missing your connection at the airport, forgetting to pack extra panties! A mistake is *not* marrying a matador!" She paused a beat, then began slowly. "I know what this is. It's a joke, isn't it? Ha ha! Right?"

Jess stared down at the naked spot on her ring finger. As soon as there was time, he'd told her, he'd buy her a big, beautiful engagement ring—and a wedding band to match. Didn't matter to him that they'd never technically been engaged.

"Jess…" Evie queried. "The silence is scaring me."

"He's not really a matador," Jess said, blinking hard. "I mean, not anymore. It's more like the family business."

"So what's this guy do?"

"He's in telecommunications."

"Hold the phone. Wait just one New York second. This couldn't possibly be…? Is it Fernando we're talking about?"

Jess felt her face flash hot.

"But you hate the guy!"

"That's just what I was saying!"

"No. You said you'd married him."

"That too."

"Hoo boy."

"Yep."

"So, what did you do? Fly to the Spanish version of Vegas?"

"More like stepped into a time warp."

"I don't understand."

"La Esperanza del Corazón, some little Spanish town near Seville."

Jess could imagine Evie massaging her forehead. While Evie often got into trouble, she very rarely got stressed. Stressing was Jess's department. "When did this happen?"

"Just last night."

"Oh, good, then it's a fresh mistake. Go out and get it undone."

"I plan to," Jess said with more resolve than she felt. "Just as soon as everything here opens back up."

"What's wrong with today?"

"It's Sunday, Evie. And tomorrow is some sort of saint day. It will be Tuesday before we can get things straightened out."

"Did you sleep with him?"

Jess hesitated a moment too long.

"Maybe a little."

"A little?"

"Okay, it was a lot. Quite a lot. Four times, to be exact."

"That's some Latin lover."

Jess sighed, reliving the heat of Fernando's caress trailing down the length of her spine.

"That good, eh?"

"I didn't say that."

"You didn't have to!"

Jess heard footsteps on the stairs. "Look Evie, I've got to run. Fernando's taking me riding."

"Not on a bull, I hope!"

"Horses, Evie," she said in hushed tones. "He's promised to explain the whole thing."

"Which thing?"

"Why he wants to keep this sham of a marriage going."

"This sounds dangerous, Jess."

"He's not dangerous, I swear. In fact, he's a very devoted son."

"*You met his mother?*"

"And she thinks I'm pregnant."

"Jess!"

She heard him approach the door and rap soundly.

"Is my new bride ready to ride?"

"Oh my God, is that him? Love the accent."

"I'll call you later," Jess whispered. "As soon as I know more!"

"Wait! Don't—"

But Jess had already pressed End Call and opened the door.

Fernando smiled at her sweetly, a bulging satchel slung over his shoulder. "I'm glad to see my sister's riding clothes fit you so well."

Her face flushed as he gave her an appreciative perusal. The fact was, they were a bit snug, but Jess had managed to struggle into them.

"What will you tell your mother about taking a woman in my condition riding?"

"I already told her what I'll now promise you." He leveled her a look with his deep green eyes, and Jess once again had that tumbling sensation. "That I would never, ever put you in danger."

Jess caught her breath, wondering for a panicked second if he'd overheard her phone conversation.

Fernando brought a hand to her face and gently stroked her cheek. "You do believe that, *querida*?"

Jess felt her heart thunder in response.

In spite of herself, she did. She was actually starting to fear she'd too easily believe just about anything Fernando told her. She was glad they were going outdoors and far from this room and its host of heated memories.

"After you," he said, gallantly stepping aside and letting her pass.

Eve pulled the ballpoint pen from her hair and anxiously thumped its cap against her desktop. *Married to a matador!* How could the normally sensible Jessica have let herself get talked into that? What was more concerning still was that she actually seemed to be considering staying in that hasty marriage. Eve turned toward her laptop and quickly pulled up a search engine, typing in *Fernando Garcia de la Vega, bullfighter*. Links for the name "Garcia de la Vega" popped up. More than two thousand results. Wow. She selected "search images," and photos of the devastatingly handsome Fernando flooded the screen. Fernando as a boy beside his equally attractive father, both dressed in full matador regalia… Fernando in the ring at twenty-two… A more mature Fernando with a gorgeous woman on his arm at an animal rights fundraiser in Madrid… What?

Eve clicked on the related story and began reading. It seemed that Fernando's grandfather had not only been one of Spain's most prized matadors, he'd also introduced a new form of "*a mano*" bullfighting in which the bull was killed cleanly with one stroke. Picadors were still present in the ring but only for show. None were allowed to injure or torment the bull. This was a game of pure skill, man versus beast, each with his own pointed weapon. One matador's blade against two deadly horns. His insistence on fighting this way had made him more than a famous matador; he'd become something of a folk hero, known for his respect for the bulls as well as his utter bravery. He'd died in the ring before the age of fifty, just as his son—Fernando's father— had, leaving behind an enormous estate.

Eve returned to the images, studying the one of Fernando as a boy who appeared to be about eight. She scanned the date of the picture, mentally calculating that Fernando must now be in his early thirties. Jessica was twenty-eight, and beautiful and talented. She hadn't had the best luck with men to date, but that didn't mean she'd have to run off and marry some guy in Spain! If Eve had the leave-time and the money, she'd get on a plane herself and talk some sense into Jess. Eve drew a deep breath, hoping that wouldn't be necessary. Eve twisted her hair back up and penned it in place. Surely, Jess would come around on her own and quickly extract herself from that *marriage by mistake*. If she didn't, Eve might just have to go begging to her boss and break out the credit card. What else on earth were best friends for?

"Jessica! Wait up!" Fernando called, galloping after her.

It had been years since she'd been on a horse, and she delighted in the freedom of the ride.

Fernando gave a loud call, and his bay Andalusian stallion picked up speed, drawing alongside Jess's gray mare.

"You are moving awfully fast for a woman in your condition." He shot her a charming grin. "Not that I'd expect anything less from a spitfire like you."

Jess slowed her horse to a trot as Fernando kept pace. "The pregnancy thing was really over the top," she said, giving him a glance. "Even for a flamboyant inventor like you."

He tilted his chin in her direction, easily reining in his horse. "I know, and I apologize for surprising you. It's just—when the idea occurred, it fit so perfectly with everything else."

"What everything else?"

He gestured to a grove of olive trees up ahead in the distance. "We'll find some afternoon shade over there. Let's stop for a while and rest the horses."

Jess was irritated he kept putting her off. She was ready for the truth and deserved it now.

Fernando dismounted, then held out his hand. She accepted his help in getting off her horse, nearly sliding into his arms. He was ruggedly handsome out here on these windswept plains, the sun dancing above them in a nearly cloudless azure sky.

"Would you mind holding this?" he asked, depositing the satchel in her arms. He withdrew a light picnic blanket from its interior and spread it beneath the craggy branches of an ancient tree.

"Won't you sit?" he said, retrieving the bag to lay it on the ground, where he knelt beside it.

Jess sat uncertainly at a safe distance, taking in the lovely landscape, the ranch, and the riding ring barely visible beyond the rolling vineyards. "How much property do you own?" she asked.

"Enough to get by," he said, uncorking the wine. "Although it's not really mine." He handed her a plastic cup filled to the brim with the lush, aromatic wine.

"It smells divine," she said, taking a sip and appreciating its full-bodied warmth and peppery finish. "Hmm. Is this one of yours?"

"A Bodega Garcia 2005. Do you like it?"

Jess more than liked it. It was fabulous, as was this place. Yet, she reminded herself, Fernando hadn't taken her into the country for some casual wine tasting. There were more serious matters at play. "It's delicious," she said, cupping her glass in both hands. "Now, your story?"

Fernando sighed, worry lines creasing his brow. "You're terribly angry with me, aren't you?"

"It takes two to tango, Fernando. I'm not saying all of this is your fault. I played a part in what happened yesterday too."

He turned toward her with a penetrating look. "That's what I don't understand. Why did you?"

Jess felt a lurch of emotion as he dissected her with his earnest green gaze. "I…don't know."

He leaned toward her with a husky whisper. "Oh, but I think you do."

He drew nearer, his mouth hovering over hers. Jess cursed herself for so badly wanting his kiss. His kisses had been so tantalizing last night, they'd made her lose all sense of reason. And it wasn't just the way he'd held her. When he'd looked deep in her eyes and said that one thing, she'd inexplicably believed him as she had no man before.

"Why did you?"

Fernando reached out and cupped her chin in his hand. "Because, *querida,* when I saw you standing there in that garden, with that beautiful smile on your lips, I knew with a certainty that I'd have to claim them. That I wouldn't rest until I made you mine."

"It was a simple sexual attraction."

"There was nothing simple about it," he said, brushing his lips to hers.

Jess closed her eyes as her heart stilled. She couldn't let herself do this, but she couldn't stop herself either. His masculine scent washed over her as she felt his palm press into the small of her back.

"Jessica," he said, resting his forehead on hers. "When I tell you the truth about this morning, I don't want you to believe that anything last night was a lie." And then to prove it, he kissed her deeply, with a skill and a passion that made her lose grip of her wine, sending the contents of her cup sloshing sideways.

"Your sister's riding pants," she said, nearly breathless.

"They'll wash," he said, tenderly stroking her thigh.

"Fernando," Jess gasped, pulling back. "We can't."

He studied her a thoughtful moment as she gazed at him wide-eyed.

"Then we won't," he said with a quick peck on her lips.

She shivered involuntarily in spite of herself. This man had a way of completely undoing her.

"We'll have a little something to eat first." He pulled several small bundles from his bag, along with a small knife and a cutting board.

"While we talk?"

"Of course," he said, handing her a napkin for her slacks. "Then afterwards, I'll let you decide."

"Decide what?"

Fernando shot her a sexy grin as he refilled her wine.

"Whether or not I'm the husband of your dreams."

End of excerpt from *How to Marry a Matador.*

Ginny Baird thanks you for reading her work and hopes to hear from you soon.